RE-ARRANGED

a novel

Ivy Daniels

REARRANGED

Copyright © 2022 Ivy Daniels

All rights reserved. No part of this book may be reproduced in any form or by any electronic or mechanical means, including information storage and retrieval systems—except in the case of brief quotations embodied in critical articles or reviews—without permission in writing from the author.

This book is a work of fiction. The characters, events, and places portrayed in this book are products of the author's imagination and are either fictitious or are used fictitiously. Any similarity to real persons, living or dead, is purely coincidental and not intended by the author.

ISBN-13: 978-1-944431-37-2

Email: authorivydaniels@gmail.com

Published in the United States of America.

Cover art @ Estella Vukovic

Other Books By Ivy Daniels

Singles in Seattle:

SUMMER IN SEATTLE

REARRANGED

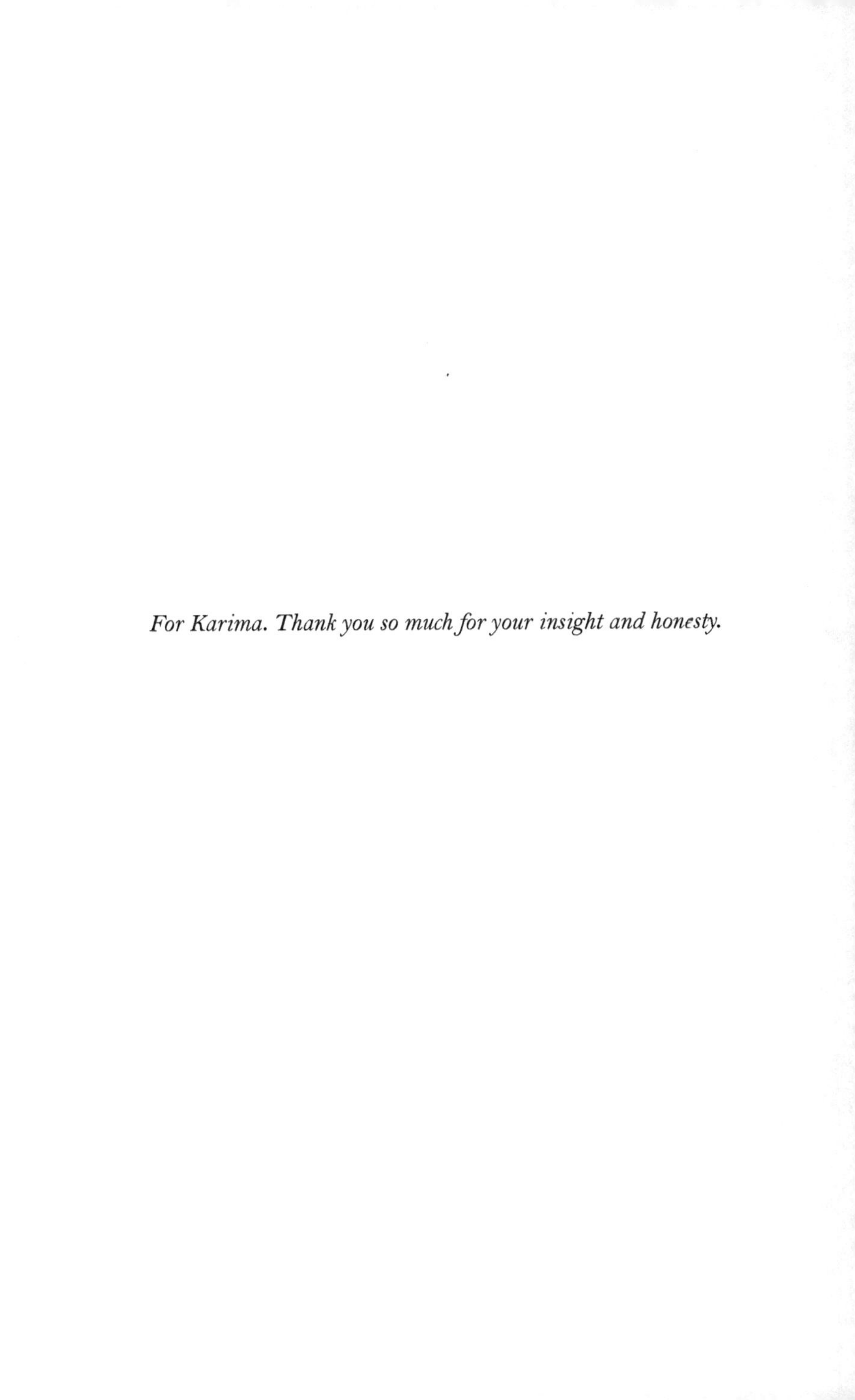

For Karima. Thank you so much for your insight and honesty.

Chapter 1

I want you so much, Eve.

I can't stop thinking about you.

You're the one who got away.

He'd said all those things to me tonight.

My dream man.

The guy I'd been obsessing over for the past eight years. Okay, more like seven and a half, but close enough. I didn't take the word *obsess* lightly either. I always felt that when it landed in the middle of a sentence—and it's a *really* big deal—it should be punctuated with a capital O. The small o is just too puny for those of us who obsessed frequently.

I was guilty as charged.

My O game was strong.

I couldn't lie. Hearing him say those words rocked my effing world. I'd been waiting for him to say that for so long. *So long!* It was a dream come true—as well as my absolute worst nightmare. Firstly, I didn't love having my world rocked. I was more of a stationary-type gal. Feet solidly planted on terra firma at all times. I liked things in their proper slots. Order was beauty. When life was unbalanced, my entire soul felt off-kilter.

Secondly, he had a fiancée.

A fiancée!

"Knock, knock, is anybody home?" Poppy asked, settling a hand on my shoulder. Poppy Albright was one of my best friends in the entire world. I'd met the most amazing three women during my freshman year in college, and trying to get through life without them would be unthinkable.

I snapped out of my daze, practically bounding off my stool, glancing around the empty storefront of my brand-new soon-to-be floral business, surprised to see that everyone else had left our kickoff celebration party. I kind of remember making my goodbyes. At least I think I did.

I'd deal with that embarrassment later.

Brushing an errant strand of red hair behind my ear, I shook my head, more than a little flustered. "Sorry. I was thinking about something else. My mind is going in a million directions these days."

To help cover my befuddlement, I hurried over to one of the tables to start tidying up. The caterers had taken all the food and dishes away, which was a relief. I wasn't up for a full clean at the moment. My brain was too busy whirring like a spin cycle stuck on Extra Panic Attack for me to tackle anything more than a simple tidy-up.

Poppy eyed me like I was an unsteady toddler. "It was a great party," she began, her tone nice and light. "Everyone had a ton of fun. The Watering Can is going to be completely amazing!

I can't wait for it to open. I'm going to buy all of my flowers here. I swear." She settled one hand over her heart and gave me a three-finger salute, making me smile. I could always count on her for that. "I won't even demand a best-friend discount." She fiddled with a red rose, rubbing a petal between her index finger and thumb. It was one of my favorite things to do. I loved the silky feel and how the scent lingered on my fingers. "Well, maybe sometimes because, you know, flowers are expensive. But most of the time, it'll be 'give me the works!'"

I laughed. "Of course you're getting the best-friend discount. Each and every time. I wouldn't have it any other way."

Realizing my dream of owning my own flower shop—an innocent wish as I'd stood next to Nana as a child, trimming beautiful long-stemmed roses and placing them in glass vases— was incredible. I had to pinch myself. This was really happening.

It was happening!

My mind should be completely focused on my new business venture. I had so much to do, order, prepare, decorate, hire. I'd sunk a ton of my blood, sweat, and tears into it already. Years of saving, scrimping, scratching, taking extra accounting jobs, trying to make ends meet while living in a tiny apartment, just so I could make my dream a reality.

But instead of being laser-focused on the task ahead, I'd allowed myself to become completely Obsessed with Marco Cruz. The urgent words he'd uttered before tugging me into the closet tonight were front and center in my cerebral cortex, like a blinking billboard in Times Square. Those words weren't going away any time soon.

It was actually *our* closet.

The man was my business partner. He'd pulled me into *our*

closet. The one we co-owned. Or co-leased. But it was still *ours* together.

Then he'd kissed me like a knight in a medieval tale of unrequited love, sweeping me back over one arm and going in for the kill. Except this love was very much requited. I'd loved him nonstop for seven and a half years, so it was quite possibly *hyper-requited.* I'd pawed at his face like a cat and lapped at his tongue like a dehydrated pony.

I'd been a goner for the man from the first time I'd laid eyes on him at the student bookstore where we'd both worked those first few months of college until right this very second.

Now my Obsession was billboard-bright.

How did I get rid of something seared into my brain by a hot, scorching kiss? A kiss I'd been waiting for my entire life.

I had no idea.

"So, um, earth to Eve. You had quite a night. Want to talk about it?" Poppy helped me stack up some extra platters I'd brought. "Annabel's getting the car, but I can have her leave without me." Poppy's sister, Annabel, had recently decided to move to Seattle. It was going to be so much fun having her around. The two of them were polar opposites in everything except personality.

There, they shone with the same dry humor and penchant for zinging, witty comebacks.

"Yeah, the party was great," I agreed, trying to recenter myself so I could start becoming an active participant in this currently one-sided conversation. "I think people had a really good time."

Poppy crossed her arms, her patience draining out of her body. The look she shot me was part Scarlett O'Hara, part

Rocky Balboa. You couldn't get past Poppy when she was on the scent of a juicy tidbit. "Eve, that's not what I'm talking about. Of course people had a good time!" She flung her arms wide. "You throw amazing parties. You always have. What I'm trying to get at is what happened in that closet midway through the festivities." She gestured toward the back of the store. "You were in there with a tall, dark, and *supremely* handsome man from your past. Who, I shouldn't have to add, is now your business partner and who has a *fiancée*. That woman was literally storming the place searching for him." Poppy dropped her arms and some of the drama, her expression easing back into that of the sympathetic pal who loved me. "What gives? This is not like you. You've always been in control—bordering on methodical—in your past relationships. I need some answers. Summer told us you had a thing for this guy freshman year, but you literally haven't mentioned him to anyone since. Things aren't adding up, and you're an accountant, for cripes' sake."

Was an accountant. Working toward becoming a flower maven.

"I need it to make sense," Poppy went on. "If I don't know the full story, I can't help you, and I want to help you."

I glanced at the door and thought about making a break for it. But it wouldn't do me any good. Poppy would hunt me down, and she'd drag Summer and Jenny with her. It would be a full-on intervention. I might as well get it out now.

"Fine. I'll tell you." I blew out a breath, resigned to spilling my guts as I sat back down on the stool, arms limp, head bowed toward the floor, which was a very pleasant light hardwood that was going to look great refinished. I loved all the dings and stains in it.

"Take your time," Poppy offered, coming to stand next to me, placing a hand on my shoulder, rubbing lightly. She was trying her best to make this easy on me. I appreciated that.

I took a fortifying inhale.

It was hard not to feel ashamed that I'd kept one of my biggest love life tidbits a secret for all this time. But I hadn't felt like I'd had much choice, so a secret it'd stayed. "I met Marco Cruz freshman year when I reported for my job study at the bookstore." I remembered that day vividly. The bright sunshine, the deep green of the Pacific Northwest, how the air had smelled vaguely floral with a hint of salt. I was so happy to finally be away at college. I'd grown up in Connecticut, and I was a long way from home. It'd already been a banner day and had only gotten better from there. "He was assigned to the same store. The exact moment I laid eyes on him, I pretty much fell completely, blindingly in love." I massaged my forehead with my fingertips. "He hit all my buttons just right. He was adorable, sweet, smart, funny. He was the fairy-tale prince from my childhood come to life. We hung out here and there in the beginning. I tried to get him to notice me in a romantic way, but failed miserably. After a month or two, he switched bookstores. I tried to make peace with the fact we weren't meant to be. It was either that or become a crazed stalker. And thankfully, the empathetic humanitarian in me wouldn't allow me to cross that line, even though my devious OCD side thought it was a spectacular idea. Wondering what he was up to all the time killed me." I closed my eyes. "I really thought the feelings I'd manufactured would go away. I mean, I hardly knew the guy. We never hooked up. He never showed any interest in me. But they never did." I'd honestly felt at some point I would forget about him—I had to. But I wasn't lying when I said I never did. "He continues to occupy my dreams, all my fantasies, and a good chunk of my day-to-day thoughts." It was exhausting at times. "It's why Brandon, Tate, and Lucas didn't work long-term. I was into them in the beginning, excited at the prospect of something new. I had high hopes they would slide right into Marco's spot. But in the end, they couldn't match my idolization of a guy I hadn't even dated." It was hard not to feel a little miserable. Poppy kept rubbing my shoulders. That was nice. "They were great guys who treated me like royalty, but they never made me *feel* like I did when I was around Marco."

"Aw, honey." Poppy hugged me against her side, jostling one of my arms up and down. "Why didn't you tell us all of this before?"

"Because I felt weak," I confessed. I hated feeling less than. I'd been raised by a strong, confident single mother to be a strong, confident woman. My obvious hang-up on Marco, something I'd been unable to shake after all this time, made me second-guess myself all the time. "I've basically been Obsessing for years over a guy who had no interest in me. Even so, I made him my *actual* pedestal—he didn't need to be up on one, he was the entire thing." I made circular motions with my hands to convey the bigness of Marco's impact on my life. "And because of that, every man I've dated hasn't stood a chance. It's dumb and pathetic and lame and just…sad." I rubbed my palms over the cute green pants I'd worn for the celebratory christening of our store. My restless energy needed an outlet. "By the time the four of us got together and became friends, I was already mourning a love that would never be. There was no reason to bring him up. We banded together to help Summer out of her heartbreak with Mitch, and since I'd never dated this guy, my own sadness seemed to pale in comparison. So I left it to fester on its own."

"You had legitimate heartbreak." Poppy rocked me back and forth. "Unrequited love counts as heartbreak. It's one of the worst kinds. Had you told us, we would've fed you treats, too. We would've tried to make you feel better. We would've showered love on you straight out of our friendship garden hose."

"I know. And I adore you for it." I laid my hand on her forearm and rested my head against her side. "But you would've told me that there were other fish in the sea. That he wasn't worthy of my love fetish, or whatever this was. That I'd get over him eventually. You would've tried to set me up with other guys. I would've felt pressure to forget him and move on. I didn't want that. The man… He…" I struggled for the right words, since Marco was an all-encompassing emotion for me instead of actual words. "He excites every single cell in my body. He always has. I feel like a massive ball of uncontrolled energy around him, and it's literally the *only* time I like to feel that way. Being out of control is not my thing. And"—I added with a sniff—"not only is he handsome, but he's completely amazing, funny, intelligent, devoted to his family, gives to charity, kind, caring… I could go on and on. I didn't want to forget about him. He's what I want in a long-term partner." I knuckled away a tear. "Now he's telling me things I've waited what feels like an eternity to hear, and I can't have him." I let go of Poppy and mopped my hands over my face, trying to dam the tide I could feel building behind my eyes. "He proposed to his live-in girlfriend recently. He's taken. I have no idea what happened here tonight, or why he decided now was the time to drag me into a closet for an epic kiss. I'm trying to figure it out, which is why it seems like I'm out of my mind. And maybe I am. It's been…a lot to handle."

"Well, damn." Poppy sighed, her arm still around me. "That was a big secret to hold on to all these years, but I understand why you kept it. We would've definitely tried to change things, distract you, set you up with a new guy. Anything to help ease the pain."

I nodded. "The only thing that made the heartbreak bearable was that he was *my* secret. My fantasy. My Obsession. I liked him taking up space in my brain. It was comforting." I sniffed, wiping the corner of my eye with a finger. My tear ducts weren't listening to me. "Up until now, that is."

"Have you kept in touch with him all this time?"

"No." Not that I hadn't tried. "I kept tabs on him through acquaintances at the bookstore during college. He dated a few girls here and there, but I lost track of him until just over a year ago. He's not on social media. We actually ran into each other at the bank, if you can believe it. It was like day one for me at the bookstore all over again. I've honestly never been so turned on by a man before or since. I almost self-destructed in the teller line. My nipples jutted to attention like two pointer puppies waiting for a treat. I acted like a complete space case, incapable of basic human communication."

"There is no way that happened," Poppy scolded, pressing her lips to the top of my head while smoothing my hair. She was going to be an excellent mother someday. "I'm sure he regretted every single day he let pass by without having you in his life. You're a feast on the eyes, Eve. Don't forget that."

I giggle-sniffed. "He was definitely not feasting. But we did end up talking for a while outside the bank. In the end, he invited me to dinner, which was a surprise. I gladly accepted, and we met a few nights later. It was wonderful to catch up. We laughed and told stories. It was perfect. Until he told me he about his live-in girlfriend." I wiped away a few more tears. Poppy made the appropriate *aww* sounds. "I pretended it was fine and that I was happy for him. That's all I could do. I told him about the floral business I was planning, and he seemed interested. He'd gotten a job at a hedge fund out of college and has done really well for himself. So, after that, we kept in touch occasionally via email. When I was ready to set the business plan in motion a month ago, I pinged him. To my surprise, he asked to meet so we could discuss it." I shrugged. "I figured if I couldn't have him in my life romantically, being partners in business would be good enough. It turned out to be a huge mistake." I shook my head, thinking about how hard I'd stumbled. "Summer warned me that night at the Driftwood when we were celebrating the business collaboration. She said we looked really into each other, but I didn't believe her. Or didn't want to. I assured—insert *fooled*—myself that everything would stay businesslike. That we were two mature adults who could handle it."

"I take it that's not what happened," Poppy murmured.

"Not at all. Sparks flew between us like a candle tossed onto an old Christmas tree. Even though my mind knew it was wrong, my body wanted it so much." That was the hardest part. "So, when he pulled me into the closet tonight, I went willingly, salivating like a lion prancing after a nice, juicy antelope. Honestly, these last few weeks have been hell." I massaged my temples. "We've been getting closer and closer, spending more and more time together, getting along amazingly, almost in perfect harmony. And it all came to a head tonight. If we hadn't acted on these feelings, we were both in danger of popping."

"Popping is not advisable." She smoothed my hair. It was keeping me grounded. "So how was the kiss, then? Worth it?"

My eyes slid closed. "Oh my, yes. It was like biting into the ripest, sweetest peach. Full and wet and soft and luscious. His lips were freaking magical." The memory of feeling them for the first time against mine shot like an arrow through my brain, causing my entire body to break out in gooseflesh. I shivered. "Far better than I ever could've imagined. We were lost in it for a while. He was slow and methodical, and I was giddy, devouring everything he gave me like a starved owlet. But as soon as it was over, I was instantly regretful." I wiped my eyes. Poppy's hand settled on my shoulder. "He has a fiancée. He hasn't tried to hide it, and he hasn't indicated he wants to break it off with her. I'm pretty sure that kiss is all we'll ever have." I glanced around my new storefront, feeling a little bewildered. "I've been brainstorming my next step. This is it for me. I hit my lowest of lows when I walked out of that closet. I'm determined to find a way to get over him, once and for all. That's where my mind has been these last few hours. This Obsession is finally coming to a close. If the Watering Can is successful, I can buy him out within a year, two at the most. Then he'll physically be out of my life forever. I'll work toward moving on emotionally after that. Until then, I'm going to avoid him by creating an iron-clad schedule that we'll both agree to abide by so our paths won't cross. He's a hands-on investor, and I need his expertise, as he's actively been involved in a few startups, but that doesn't mean I have to be in the same room with him. I'm not a homewrecker." The last word came out on a sob. I rubbed my shirtsleeve under my nose, uncaring about manners at this point. "Even though he's my deepest fantasy"—I sniffed—"I will not be responsible for breaking up his relationship with Yasmine. I don't want to hurt her."

"Come on, stand up. Give me a hug," Poppy ordered as she stepped back and opened her arms.

I stood and embraced her, my head dipping comfortably onto her shoulder. I was almost a foot taller, but we made it work. I always forgot how tiny she was.

"It's going to be okay. I promise it is," she cooed softly. "We'll find a way to deal with this together, like we always do. I'm not going to promise it's going to be easy, but I know you can get over him if you set your mind to it. You're one of the strongest people I know. Of course you're not a homewrecker. Nobody thinks that."

The front door whooshed open, and Annabel burst in, taking in the scene. "Okay, um, what's happening? Did somebody die?"

"I'm giving my friend some comfort," Poppy said, shushing Annabel as I raised my head. "Give us a minute."

Annabel gestured toward the street. "I totally would, but there's an aggressive dude who wants my parking space. He's resorted to hand gestures that aren't very polite. And, you know"—she brought her phone up to flash the time—"I've given you, like, a thousand minutes already. I've been waiting out there for an hour."

"Fine, fine. We're ready," Poppy announced, detaching from our hug.

I tried to fix my hair, knowing I probably looked like hell. I brushed away any liquid stuck to my cheeks, paying close attention to the finger swipes under my eyes to get rid of runny makeup.

"Change of plans. I'm sending you on an errand," Poppy said to Annabel. "We need a large pepperoni pizza—extra cheese, extra pepperoni—and a pint of double chocolate ice cream, stat. A fancy brand, not one of those cheapy tub ones." She waggled her finger. "We'll meet you at Eve's place once you have the goods."

"You don't have to do that, Annabel," I told her, ashamed that she was being ordered to take care of me. "Your sister's just trying to be nice. I don't want you to run errands."

Annabel snorted. The sound was equal—to the note—to her sister's. Dainty, precise, and to the point. "Nice try, but you're not escaping an emotional intervention with that tyrant in charge." She gestured at Poppy, who huffed, then giggled. "I'm happy to do the running. It's no hassle. And, I mean, it's clear you need a pick-me-up. I'll see you both in thirty."

I lived a few blocks from Poppy in Capitol Hill. Annabel already knew her way around the city. "I'm assuming the pizza has to come from Giovanni's?"

"No—" I started.

"Of course it has to be from Giovanni's," Poppy snapped. "Have I taught you nothing?"

"Fine, but I'm charging that guy for my parking space. He owes me."

Chapter 2

There was no interfering with Poppy when she was on a mission. Annabel was completely right. A drill sergeant with a stern demeanor couldn't deter her, and I was mostly grateful for it. Being alone tonight would've been hard.

After cleaning up the shop a little, we Ubered to my apartment in Capitol Hill. I lived in a plain, unimaginative, five-story, concrete building built sometime in the seventies, updated once in the nineties. The apartment was cheap, and that was all I cared about.

Overall, it was fine. Dingy, but fine.

I opened the door and switched on the lights, setting my purse on the small table by the door. "I took your advice and got some of those adhesive mirrors." I indicated my living room. "You were right. They made a huge difference. The space definitely feels bigger."

Poppy was a talented interior designer. I was happy she was

getting back into it. She'd never really elaborated on why she'd left the big, swanky company she'd worked for a few years ago, other than being generally dissatisfied. Summer's new boyfriend, Xander, and Leo and Chris, his business partners, had recently hired her to design the interior of their craft brewery. She was insanely excited, sharing ideas with us constantly. It was fun to see her thriving. Not to mention seeing her interest in Leo and their budding romance.

"The mirrors look great," she said, moving into the room. "I see you got some multicolored throw pillows, too. They look fantastic against all this beige." Poppy walked around, inspecting.

I chuckled as I hung my coat on a peg next to the door. "I like beige. It's comforting."

"That may be true, but if you don't add a pop of color here and there, it's too drab."

"So you've mentioned."

"Only trying to help," she chirped. "Just like when you help me with my taxes. Your accountant brain is big and vast." Poppy plopped down on my couch. "My designer brain is equally vast, so we share. This thing is incredibly comfy, though"—she caressed the top of the couch—"despite its color."

I'd made a safe choice. No regrets.

My sofa had been my biggest expenditure thus far. That and my mahogany bedframe. I'd allowed myself to splurge on only a few things over the years, and I was glad, because look where I was. *A small-business owner!* The scrimping had been worth it.

"Do you want a drink?" I asked as I walked into my kitchen. It was galley-style—a counter and a sink on one side, a long rectangular cutout to the living room you had to duck your head to use on the other. It was in no way an open floor plan. Someday.

"Water's fine. You had some rockin' champagne at the party, and I had two glasses, which is my limit tonight. I'm meeting Leo tomorrow morning at the pub." Excitement peppered her voice. "I need to be on point."

"That's fantastic. Do you think he'll finally get up the courage to ask you out?" I opened my fridge, which was a dismal cream color, and took out a bottle of white wine, pouring myself a glass. Then I pulled out a jug of cold water.

"I have no idea. The man is an enigma. A beautiful, fastidious, gorgeous-eyed enigma who has excellent taste in blazers."

Taking my Pinot Grigio and her glass of water, I joined her in the living room, handing her drink to her. I perched on the other end of my large couch, grabbing my phone out of my pocket and setting it on a cushion between us. Poppy was right that my sofa was incredibly comfortable. I spent a lot of downtime here. My living room flowed into an L space that could've been used as a dining room, but I'd set up my office there instead. I had a teensy second bedroom, but it was too claustrophobic to work in there all day. The full-sized bed I'd put in there for guests took up most of the space.

I was a freelance accountant slash bookkeeper with a decent client list. I'd done well for myself and was proud of my achievements thus far. With my new business taking shape, I'd given my clients three months' notice that I'd be decreasing my hours. Most of my clients had taken it well. One of the small companies decided to stay on with me, and one went in a different direction, which was actually perfect.

Poppy glanced up from her phone. "Annabel just texted. She

has the pizza and is stopping for ice cream. She should be here in ten." She set her device on my square, walnut-stained coffee table, a valued Craigslist purchase.

I loved Craigslist. It'd been my savior.

"Is there anything you want to talk about before she gets here?"

I took a sip of my wine. "Like what? I just bared my soul to you. I have nothing left to tell. That was my one and only secret. I swear." I flashed her the same three-finger salute she'd given me back at the store and smiled.

"Oh, come on. I'm sure there're still a few lingering tidbits hiding in there." She grinned. "What I mean is, we don't have to discuss your love life in front of my sister if you're not comfortable sharing."

I swished a hand. "I'm fine with Annabel knowing. It's out in the ether, and there's nothing I can do to pull it back in. Summer and Jenny are going to hear about it soon." I didn't want to think about that. They were both going to feel bad thinking they could've helped me all these years. I took another drink of my nice, chilled wine. I'd splurged on a more expensive bottle than usual, in the ten-dollar range, and it was good. Not the best I'd had, but decent. "What I really wish is that I'd figured out how to forget that man long before now." I closed my eyes briefly. "Marco's been living in my brain rent-free since the day I first laid eyes on him, but I've never made a move to actively forget him. He's my sexy pacifier. Anytime I need a hit, I just pop it in and take a suck." I shook my head. "But I can't continue to foster the ideal of what a man should be with an imaginary love affair. It's come between all of my real relationships. My brain needs to be rewired to be Marco-free." I blew out a breath.

"Do they still do shock therapy?"

"You don't need to be rewired," Poppy said. "We all have sexy pacifiers we like to, um, suck on." She giggled. "I just rotate guys in. If I'm feeling like it's a Chris Hemsworth night, I go there. If I feel like it's a Bradley Cooper night, he stops by. Lately, Chris Evans has been a crowd-pleaser. His paci tastes mighty fine. Celebrities are convenient, but only because I haven't yet experienced that deep connection with someone like you have. If I had, I'm sure that guy would be front and center during all of my happy yum-yum time." I snorted. "And if you want to talk about unhealthy relationships, let's talk about Michael for a second." Poppy's last boyfriend had been controlling and hard to get rid of. "I was convinced things were fine because I basically rewrote our entire relationship in my mind from day one. I'd been dating this guy for two years, and it took all of you, over multiple interventions, to get me to see what was really going on. That he was isolating me away from the people I loved. That he was controlling our relationship. I was stubborn. I didn't want to let him go. A lot of time, our hearts just want what they want. There's no shame in that."

"At least yours was a real guy," I pointed out, drinking more wine. My stomach gurgled. I was actually hungry. I hadn't eaten a single bite at the party. For Obvious reasons. "It makes it more pathetic that I kept feeding a fake relationship and then held real men to the impossible standard I created."

"Not pathetic at all," Poppy said. "I was dating a real guy while rewriting the relationship in my mind. I manufactured something happy in my brain, made it pleasant and agreeable. I knew Michael's personality was flawed. On our very first date, he ordered my meal for me! No one does that. I don't even like baked fish! I just thought I could mold him into the exact kind of partner I wanted. He was sexy and fun. He had a lot of good qualities." She shrugged, taking a sip of her water. "Then, when reality finally conflicted with my fantasy, I still didn't ditch him. I tried to fix him. I felt like if I was successful, then we'd *finally* fall into this manic, moony love, and everything would be fine. I just needed to apply a little elbow grease." She mocked running her hands up and down an old-timey washboard while sticking her tongue out one side of her mouth and crinkling her brows.

I giggled.

"So, how's that for fantasizing?" she asked. "I'm a walking, talking relationship trope. The heroine who heroically fixes the broken hero so they can live happily ever after." She shrugged. "But I'm pretty certain that guy doesn't exist. When your partner shows you who he is, believe him the first time. Broken usually stays broken." She sat back on the couch, crossing her ankles. "But I try not to feel too bad about it. We're fed relationship perfection day in and day out from the time we're born. Every Disney princess finds her perfect match. It makes sense that we'd cleave to these fantasies in our minds. But that's all they are, fantasies. Being hyperfocused on Marco and how he made you feel aided your notion of what a perfect relationship means to you. You weren't ready to hear this before, but there are other guys out there who will fill that role. Not perfection, because nobody has that." Poppy gave me a knowing look. "I'm not going to harp on it, but when the time is right, you'll open yourself up to it, and it will happen."

I sighed. "Intellectually, I know you're right. I'll be ready at some point, but emotionally I'm nowhere near there now." I drank the last of the wine and set the glass on the coffee table.

"Okay, enough about me and my fake boyfriend. What about you and Leo? He seems like a great guy. Does he make your heart go pitter-patter?"

Poppy's face broke out into a huge grin. "Oh yeah. My heart feels like it's going to explode right out of my chest when I'm around him. I'm so ridiculously attracted to him. He's giving Chris Evans a run for his money." She winked and pressed the palm of her hand over her heart. "But because of what happened with Michael, I'm feeling…I don't know…shy? It's weird, because I'm so extroverted." That was not a lie. "I've been the instigator with every guy I've ever dated, up until now. But I'm okay with Leo taking the lead. Even though he hasn't picked up the reins yet." She drew out an exaggerated sigh. "It's been hard not to point-blank ask him out, but I'm also enjoying the slow burn. I'm a walking contradiction, so take what I say with some caution. I could change my mind at any moment."

"He'll make his move soon. I'm sure of it."

"Summer told me he just got out of a six-year relationship with a woman named Pamela. He hasn't mentioned her. If she broke his heart, he probably needs more time to recover before he makes his move. Either that, or he thinks I'm an annoying, crazy lady he can't wait to ditch once our business partnership is over. That is a distinct possibility." She chuckled. "I recently found this amazing wallpaper and want to switch gears from our working plan. He's worried about it. But if the guys take my advice, the bar is going to be amazing. I can't wait for you guys to see it!"

"I can't wait either," I told her sincerely. I knew it would be awesome. "I'm sure Leo doesn't think you're a crazy lady. When you two are together, nobody else exists. He's completely into you. Maybe he's waiting for a stronger signal? He strikes me as kind of a shy guy, too."

Poppy snorted right as my buzzer sounded, indicating Annabel was downstairs, waiting to be let in. I stood, moving toward the intercom. It was one of those chunky, off-white boxes that had yellowed with age and had hard-to-push buttons. It definitely hadn't been updated since the seventies.

"A stronger signal?" Poppy cackled from the living room. "That would mean I'd have to perform a Fred Flintstone maneuver and bang him over the head with my trusty club. I've all but climbed into the guy's lap. I've worn V-necked shirts down to my navel. I've sprayed on my killer, man-snaring perfume, which I call Eau de Pure Sex. But oddly, it's kind of endearing that he's taking his time. He does seem really engaged when we're together. He'll ask me out when he's ready. Or maybe he won't. Either way, we'll be friends for life. I'm sure of that."

I buzzed Annabel in without checking to see if it was her. The intercom had an ear-piercing reverberation I didn't care for.

So either a serial killer or Annabel would be up soon.

Then I headed into the kitchen to get plates for the pizza and spoons for the ice cream. Poppy came in to help, grabbing a glass for Annabel and some napkins. She knew where everything was. She'd been here a million times. I loved that about all my friendships. We were all comfortable in one another's homes.

A rap sounded on the door. Poppy opened it with a dramatic whoosh. "Finally! I thought you went clubbing instead." She took the pizza out of Annabel's hand and carried it straight into the living room.

"Clubbing? Did we teleport back to the early nineties while I was gone?" Annabel entered the kitchen, setting the ice cream on the counter.

"I've got clubs on the brain," Poppy called. "Long story."

"I would've been here earlier," Annabel said, "but finding a decent place to park was the hardest part of this entire endeavor. I finally snagged a spot a block away. Oh, and Hand Gesture Guy sends his love. He can't wait to buy flowers from the Watering Can. I told him if he didn't do it weekly, I'd hunt him down on social media and out him for harassing me." She giggled maniacally. "For some reason, he believed me. I have no idea why. I have zero clue what his name is. It's not like I can track him down by the make and model of his car. But he seemed pretty nervous, so I hope he becomes a decent human being and stops in."

"That'll teach him to mess with you," I told her, giving her a quick hug. "Thanks so much for picking all this up."

Annabel was a little taller than I was, and I was five eight. Her thick chestnut hair had a perfect natural wave and hung past her shoulders. She was tall and athletic like her father, which was the polar opposite of Poppy, who was petite and blonde. No one would pick them out as sisters in a crowd, and they absolutely loved it.

"That's my girl," Poppy said, coming into the kitchen. "Give 'em hell, that's what I always say."

"Are you kidding?" Annabel laughed. "Your go-to in a stressful situation is to flee the scene with your hands flailing over your head like a Muppet."

"I may act Muppety if given a choice, but I can throw a mean punch if backed into a corner."

"True," Annabel admitted. "I've been on the receiving end of a few of those."

"Lucky for you, my prizefighting days are over. That and you stopped stealing my favorite sweaters and my best lip gloss," Poppy said. "Come on. The pizza is in the living room. Grab the ice cream. Even though I ate a healthy amount at the party—and let me tell you, those stuffed mushrooms were to *die for*—I'm starving all of a sudden."

"I'm hungry, too," I said. We followed her into the living room and threw my new multicolored pillows on the floor. They made nice butt cushions. The coffee table was pretty much my only dining location if I didn't want to eat at my desk or stand up in my kitchen. "Yum, this looks so good. Giovanni's is the *best*."

"They gave me a bunch of coupons." Annabel reached into her pocket and set a handful of paper strips on the table. She shrugged. "I guess they didn't have anything better to do at eleven thirty p.m. on a Thursday, so they plied me with them." She reached over and snagged a piece of pizza, the cheese stretching the entire way to her plate.

"You're always getting free stuff," Poppy groused, grabbing her own slice. "No fair. They treat me like a grandma when I'm there."

I laughed while taking my own piece. "What are you talking about? One of their servers has been trying to get up the courage to ask you out for ages. He gives you those puppy-dog eyes, practically begging you to notice him every time we go."

"That Dimitri guy?" Poppy took a bite and moaned. "This is *sooo* good." She wiped her chin with a napkin. "He's easily forty-five and has been divorced twice. That's a hard pass."

"Not him." I took a moment to chew the deliciousness. Giovanni's was definitely the best pizza I'd ever had in my life.

We'd lived on it in college, and it still hadn't gotten old. "The other one. The short guy with the slicked-back hair. He has an Italian accent. You love accents! I'm surprised you two haven't hooked up, actually. You'd look totally cute together." I took another scrumptious bite.

"Oh, Italian Fabio?" Poppy snorted. "I think his name is Rafael. I do love his accent. Yeah, we've definitely flirted through the years, but he's never given me a fistful of coupons. So, you know, he can't love me that much."

We ate the yummy pizza until we were full. Then Poppy popped the top off the pint of dark chocolate ice cream and dug a spoon in, pulling out a heaping scoop and holding it out to me.

I groaned, rubbing my stomach. "I don't think I have room. We decimated that pie." There was only a piece and a half left.

"This is nonnegotiable. It's your medicine." She waved the spoon in slow circles in front of me. "It demands to be eaten. The sugar and extra-rich chocolate will make you forget your own name. That's what we're striving for here. We want you in a complete delirium so nothing can penetrate the fog, and the only way to do that is to ingest it."

Admitting defeat, I took it from her, opening my mouth wide and placing the entire bite inside. I tugged the spoon out slowly, leaving the remains of a creamy molded mound. "Oh yeah." My eyes fluttered close. "That hits the *spot*."

"See? That's the delirium talking. It's totally working." Poppy handed a spoonful to Annabel, who brought it up to her nose and sniffed. Poppy looked appalled. "What the hell? Why would you *sniff* ice cream?"

Annabel shrugged. "I sniff just about everything. It's a habit."

"Since when?" Poppy demanded.

"Since right this second, when I wanted to know if this ice cream smells like hot chocolate." Annabel popped the tip of the spoon into her mouth and bit off a sizable chunk, savoring it. "Because I know what your next question will be, no, it doesn't smell like hot chocolate. It just smells cold."

Poppy shook her head, pretending to be put out. "See what I have to deal with? Ice cream sniffers, that's who."

My phone chimed from its position on the couch.

Our heads turned toward it, none of us speaking.

It was Marco's tone.

Everybody had an assigned ringtone in my phone, as I found it easier to discern whether I should answer while I was working. It was much easier to decide if I knew who was texting or calling me. It's called being Organized.

"So, um, are you going to grab that?" Annabel asked. "Or should I? I'm happy to chuck it out the window if you'd like." She was the closest to the phone, her back resting against the couch.

"That's kind of you, but I'll get it." I leaned over her shoulder to reach for it.

"That's Marco, isn't it?" Poppy asked. "Do you want me to prescreen the text?"

I shook my head, taking a breath. "No, I've got it."

Hugging my phone to my chest, I sat back down. I could do this. It's not like I wasn't going to have to talk to this man again. We had business meetings together all week. That was, until I revised the schedule.

Before I could draw the phone away to look, Poppy jumped up, calling, "Wait!" She ran into the kitchen.

I glanced over at Annabel. "What's she doing?"

"I've known her my *entire* life, and I have no frickin' idea. If she thinks my ice cream sniffing is weird, she hasn't looked in the mirror lately." Annabel dipped her spoon back into the ice cream, grinning. "This stuff is really good. I had no idea. I'm more of a cookies-and-cream gal myself." She took another bite, her eyelids fluttering shut.

Poppy came rushing back with a saltshaker that she thrust into my hand. "Use this first," she commanded.

I glanced down at the crystal shaker that had been my nana's, confused. "What am I supposed to do with it?"

"Toss some over your shoulder for luck," she replied. "It's supposed to undo all the bad stuff. Don't ask questions, just do it." She prodded me on with a flick of her wrist.

I chuckled. "Are you telling me that throwing salt over my shoulder is going to negate me making out with a man, who has a fiancée, in a closet during a party celebrating my lifelong dream of becoming a shop owner in front of a passel of beloved family and friends? Does this saltshaker turn back time?" What I wouldn't give.

"No, silly. It's for luck. After the dash of salt, you're going to find out he's been in love with you all along and plans to leave his fiancée because it was a bad idea to get engaged in the first place. This saltshaker is going to solve all your problems. I have a good feeling about this!" She clapped her hands.

I glanced at Annabel, who lofted her eyebrows. "When you're done, hand it to me," she quipped dryly.

"I'm pretty certain you've lost your mind," I told Poppy. "But I'm going to placate you because you're asking so sweetly." I flicked a couple shakes of salt over my shoulder.

The only thing I knew for sure was I'd be vacuuming in the morning. My stick vacuum was the absolute bomb. These tiny grains of salt wouldn't stand a chance.

I handed the saltshaker to Annabel and brought my phone out in front of me, tapping the screen.

"What does it say?" Poppy urged. "I can't stand the suspense."

Instead of telling her, I flipped the phone around so she could read it.

WE NEED TO TALK.

Chapter 3

Much to my disappointment, the saltshaker hadn't turned back time. Stuck in the here and now, the three of us finished the pint of ice cream and discussed a bunch of appropriate responses for me to reply to Marco.

I'd argued for simply getting a new phone and avoiding all contact, but I was overruled. It really wasn't realistic, since Marco and I had commitments together, and he had to have my number.

Then I'd argued for pretending the whole thing hadn't happened. I'd explain to Marco that he'd had some sort of psychotic break, and the two women sitting next to me would back me up completely.

Also overruled.

In the end, I'd settled on texting him one word.

OK.

To which he'd immediately responded:

GREAT. I'LL STOP BY IN THE MORNING BEFORE MY DAY JOB.

I'd panicked a quantifiable amount after that.

With patience and supreme nurturing, Poppy and Annabel had calmed me down, assuring me I would be capable of getting through a one-on-one meeting with Marco in my living room in the morning. That we weren't going to have crazy cheetah sex on my comfy couch, using a multicolored throw pillow as a hip positioner, the moment he walked through the door.

That, as two mature adults, we could agree that something like the closet incident would never happen again. To further facilitate this agreement, in the future when we had to see each other, we would meet in a coffee shop or some otherwise crowded location.

It all sounded very sane and ordered. Just the way I liked it.

However, I'd just gotten out of the shower, and I was feeling a little wobbly kneed. It was eight a.m., and Marco would be here soon. I felt myself entering into full-on washer-spin-cycle Panic Attack territory. If left to my own devices, I would eventually make my way into hyperventilation territory.

My phone chimed from its spot on my vanity. It was Poppy's tone. I picked it up for fortification.

you can do this. no panicking! he'll be in and out quickly.

Three dots popped up immediately, followed by:

bad choice of words. what i meant to say is you will solve this, and all will be fine. promise! hit me when you're done.

I set the phone down without answering. I had nothing to share with her yet. If I told her I was about to lock myself in my bedroom, pull the covers over my head, and try to reimagine my life as a geologist in Alaska, she would race over. I didn't want that. Poppy running was an incredible thing to see, but not today. I knew she was at the ready to spring into action, and I appreciated it. It was enough.

Dressing quickly, I finished drying my hair, which was always a bit of an ordeal since it was thick. I'd decided on a casual work outfit—jeans and a button-up shirt. So what if my cerulean-blue top with the plunging vee made my long red hair pop and sparkle?

I wasn't trying to be sultry. This was a comfortable shirt.

Crap, maybe I should change?

No, he's almost here! He's allowed to see what he's missing!

That felt extremely counterproductive and childish, but I was going to let my inner heartbreak have its way. In fact, every time I saw him in the future, I might dress to the nines. Why not? It was probably time to schedule a haircut, too. I'd neglected doing that for a long time because it was expensive. My hair was long, and a little boring, but some fresh layers might bounce it up nicely. It was also time to visit that secondhand-couture handbag shop I loved. Why not?

Get your head in the game! He'll be here soon.

The reason for this meeting wasn't to try to make him jealous. It was about righting the wrongs that'd happened last night and making sure they didn't happen again. And to look my absolute best while doing it.

For the love of everything human, shut this line of thinking down and get it together already!

I didn't have time to shut anything down, because my intercom buzzed.

It was reckoning time, and I hadn't even had a chance to have a cup of coffee yet, which was probably for the better. Adding more jitters on top of all the other jitters wasn't advisable.

My intercom buzzed again, and I green-lit Marco up without using the speaker.

He'd been here several times over the last few weeks to sign papers solidifying our business agreement. It'd been the easiest place to do things because this was my office.

Now I felt a little bad, thinking his fiancée might not like him coming over here so much. I hadn't even thought of her before, having faith in my undying professionalism.

So much for that crap. I'd failed miserably.

A knock sounded on the door.

I froze. I wasn't ready. I didn't want to talk about my misgivings like a rational adult. I just wanted it all to go away!

None of this was going to evaporate into thin air, so I did the only thing I could do and opened the door.

Only, Marco wasn't standing there. Yasmine, his fiancée, was.

My mouth literally tumbled open in shock. I was too startled to form coherent thoughts.

"Hello, Eve."

"Um, hi, Yasmine. Nice to see you." We'd met a few times, including seeing each other last night. We hadn't exactly had a conversation, but we had exchanged pleasantries.

I shuffled back, allowing her to enter my apartment. Once inside, she made her way into my living room. I followed, eyeing her uneasily.

This couldn't be good, could it?

My heart was beating a million miles per hour. It felt like it might burst out of my chest like a thoroughbred crossing the finish line at the Kentucky Derby.

She glanced around. "Well, this is…adequate. I pictured you

living in a much nicer place. You're always so put together." She seemed disappointed, which was strange.

"Yeah, it's not exactly fancy." I cleared my throat, trying to find the appropriate words to string together to make an intelligent sentence. "The rent here is cheap. It's allowed me to save money." I shrugged. "It's been worth it."

"You're probably wondering why I'm here instead of Marco."

I was wondering exactly that.

In response, I nodded.

"I texted you from his phone. I know about the two of you."

For a hot second, I said nothing.

Then I began to stammer, trying not to clutch at my neck or begin a rapid-breathing cycle that would bring on a bout of paper bag-worthy hyperventilating. "We aren't… We didn't… I mean, we…" My shoulders slumped. "I'm *so* sorry, Yasmine. It was wrong of us to sneak off together last night. I was going to tell him that today. It was only a kiss. I swear to you it'll never happen again." I held up my hand like I was readying to swear an oath in court. All I needed was the Good Book to be placed in front of me. Or for someone to hit me in the head with it. "I'm extremely ashamed of what we did. Nothing more has gone on between us. You have my word. We're not…having an affair or anything like that." It was hard to get the words out, but it was incredibly important that she understood where things stood.

She swished a perfectly manicured hand through the air.

Her long, cherry-red nails matched her wool trench perfectly. She looked radiant and utterly confident in her right to be in my living room talking about her fiancé. "I know you're not sleeping together. I'm aware of everything. Marco's been upfront with me about his feelings for you as they've grown. I knew last night was a possibility."

Marco told her about me? What does that mean?

"I'm here, not because I'm upset or angry, but to explain a few things. Then I have a proposition for you, because without your help, I'm not sure I can pull it off by myself."

My knees basically gave out.

A proposition?

Luckily, I was in front of a chair. I collapsed into it with an unladylike *thump*. "Okay," I croaked, *aheming* to clear my airway. "I'm listening."

She unbelted her coat and tossed it over the back of the sofa. Her long, dark hair tumbled down around her shoulders, highlighting a seafoam-green sweater paired with black jeans. She took a seat directly across from me. "Just so you know, my relationship with Marco was arranged by our families. It's why we're together. I don't think he's shared that information with you, has he?"

He hadn't.

"No," was all I could manage.

"It's not something we offer up freely, for reasons you can probably imagine. Arranged marriages are not common in the US, particularly involving two Americans. People here can be incredibly judgy, especially when it pertains to cultures and traditions they know nothing about, nor do they wish to learn. I love being Moroccan-American, and the rich heritage it brings. I wouldn't change it for the world." She folded her hands across her knee. Her movements were elegant, and she seemed completely at ease. "And, in case you're curious, the arrangement was made with our blessing. It's a modern agreement, and we have the power to veto it if we choose. We did it because we love and respect our parents and would essentially move heaven and earth for them. Not to mention, many of our extended family members have had successful unions set up this way, including both my grandparents and Marco's. So we said yes. We were, of course, hoping it would lead to a love match."

I had little knowledge on the subject. No one I knew had an arranged marriage. I'd, of course, heard about them and knew they were very common throughout the world.

With one eyebrow subtly arched, she flashed a smile. She knew this was not what I'd expected to hear this morning. "Moving on," she continued. "I'm going to give you the entire story because I think it'll be easier that way." That sounded ideal. "Once we both agreed to an introduction, Marco and I got to know each other slowly. We communicated over the phone, email, and video chat. This went on for about three or four months. During that time, we grew fond of one another. It's hard not to fall for Marco because he's such a nice guy." I knew exactly what she was talking about. "After the initial get-to-know-you phase, we agreed to move forward with the arrangement, so I uprooted my life in Boston and moved across the country to be with him. We were both full of hope for the future." She recrossed her legs and readjusted herself on the couch, inclining her head politely as if to inquire if I had any questions thus far.

I had quite a few, but I was going to ask only one. I tried not to sound pitiful. "Did you fall in love?"

If they were in love, not only was I embarrassed that I'd followed Marco into the closet like an eager puppy, but I was about to be very angry at him for all the flirting and closeness that had been happening between us since we'd become business partners. He had not acted like a man in love.

"No, which is one of the reasons I'm here," Yasmine clarified.

Relief swept through me. I was still mortified that we'd kissed in the first place, but it felt better to know that his vibe toward me had been real.

"As I prefaced, we were both hopeful it would work out, and we would fall madly, blindingly in love." Her smile held a hint of wistfulness. "That would've solved a lot of issues. For one, I wouldn't be here, as I'd already be happily married." She idly brushed her fingertips along the couch cushion next to her, lost in thought for a moment. "We started off slowly, in separate bedrooms. We went on dates and all that. I don't want to give you the impression that I jumped into his bed without knowing him. He was nothing but a gentleman, willing to go at my pace." She met my gaze. "But at the end of the day, we're two very different people. I'm social and outgoing and love to take risks, which is probably why I agreed to this in the first place, and he's more introverted and cautious, which is why it's taken us so long to figure this out. And the fact is"—she uncrossed her legs—"we couldn't make a love connection no matter how hard we tried. And, believe me, we gave it a very good go." She flashed a wry grin. "Then he met you, and everything began to change." My heart threatened to stop beating right then and there. "Or, I should say, he remet you, because you two went to college together, right?"

"We did." Embarrassingly, the words came out in a croak. A frog the size of a zebra had lodged in my throat because my adrenaline hose would *not* stop chugging through my body. I was completely hopped up. I coughed into my fist. "I'm sorry. I'm having trouble getting words out. I met him at the bookstore we both worked at the first few months of freshman year. Then he switched bookstores, and I didn't see him again." *But I thought about him every waking moment. Does that count?* "Until last year, when we ran into each other at the bank."

"You guys had dinner together."

My eyes widened. I resisted pawing at my throat. Was it closing now? It felt like it was closing. "Yes. But I promise nothing happened."

"Oh, I know. Marco and I didn't make a love match, but we basically became best friends. When you sent him the email detailing your business venture last month, we discussed it. He was pretty excited because all your numbers looked really good. He's made a lot of money at his hedge fund and loves seeding new startups. It's a real passion for him. I had an inkling at that time that he might end up falling for you, as he'd gushed about the profound impact you had on his life. So I encouraged him to invest." She shrugged like that information was no big deal. "We needed to see where it would lead."

"I had an impact…on his life?" *And it was profound?*

That was news to me.

I'd aggressively flirted with him, and he'd changed bookstores. I would've categorized my impact as less than optimal.

"I'll leave that for him to explain later." She stood, making her way to my very serviceable windows with a view of a crowded Seattle street. "I encouraged Marco to go into business with you, hoping he might fall in love or at least figure out what he wants." She glanced over her shoulder, grinning. "I know that sounds weird. I'm sure you weren't expecting to hear any of this."

I hadn't. Not in the least. Like, furthest from my mind type of thing.

She turned and walked back toward the couch. "But my plan worked, and now that you two clearly have feelings for each other, Marco and I can formally break our engagement." She sat, this time leaning forward. "And, just so you know, we'd already broken up before the party last night, so he wasn't cheating on me. But telling our family is another story. We'll need to do it thoughtfully so no offense is given. If my plan works, everyone should be happy. And if they're not happy, then they're at least content."

CHAPTER 4

I was lost in thought for a few moments. Yasmine and Marco were broken up, and Yasmine thought Marco and I had a future together.

The thought of being with Marco made me giddy with excitement. I'd been waiting for this for so long.

Yasmine cleared her throat.

Snapping back to reality, I realized that I'd been less than a gracious hostess and asked, "Can I offer you coffee or water or anything?"

She shook her head, pulling her phone out of her jacket pocket and glancing at the screen. "I can't stay. I have to be to work in thirty. Let me tell you the rest, and I'll get out of your hair. You can give me your answer to my proposition later."

I could not imagine what she was going to suggest.

She set her phone on the cushion beside her and continued, "The reason we have to tread carefully regarding telling our families is because when Marco proposed two months ago, it solidified our union in a new way. It made it real for our families. There was a lot of joyous celebration. Parties were thrown for us. It basically made the contract real." She arranged her long, dark hair behind her ears. "After the proposal, we knew we'd made a mistake. Up until that point, we'd been living in a sort of pretend euphoria. High on the *idea* of love, but not really experiencing it between the two of us. It's hard to explain unless you've gone through it." She waved a hand in front of her. "Which you won't, so you'll have to take my word for it. But within a week or two, after everything had sunk in, we were both feeling some heavy regret. People who grow up in America idealize love. Finding that *one* person who is your perfect match seems like everyone's quest from birth. And if I'm being truthful, I mourned that neither of us was going to get that. I think he did, too." She ran a hand through her hair. I could tell this part was more emotional for her, so I waited patiently for her to finish. "But we both felt stuck and committed to what we had decided. Then, a month or so after our engagement, he entered into the business agreement with you, and you two started spending a lot of time together. I immediately saw a change in him. He was full of joy and more content than he'd been in a long time. I saw passion in him I hadn't seen before. I was truly happy for him. I knew at this point that we would be parting ways, which honestly, we would've ended up doing at some point even if you hadn't come along. It just happened sooner because you were in the picture. For me, seeing that change in Marco was a necessary catalyst. Knowing for certain that we could both marry for love was cathartic, even though I knew in here"—she tapped the side of her head—"I had to feel it here"—she placed a palm over her heart.

What she was saying was moving me in a way I hadn't anticipated. I didn't want to settle for anything less than a love match either. She deserved a happy ending just as much as I did. And Marco. And everyone else.

"Now I know, without a doubt, I *will* marry for love and have a richer experience for it." Her smile held a hint of sadness. "The only problem is both of our families are heavily invested in our union. These marriage contracts, even a modern one, carries weight." She recentered a beautiful gold necklace on her neck. It was a small disk with the imprint of the sun. "There's bound to be some offense and hard feelings, especially if Marco moves on quickly with someone else." She paused, cocking her head, her dark hair flowing over her shoulder as she flashed a wry smile. "Then I discovered some interesting news that I'm completely excited about. It could change things moving forward."

I literally couldn't wait to hear what it was. I was on board to facilitate whatever she needed. Helping her sounded to me like it would be a very win-win situation.

"This news pertains to my ex-boyfriend, Matt Gallagher. I never, ever thought I'd get a second chance with him, but one of my close friends thinks he might still be interested in me." Her phone beeped, and she picked it up, quickly checking the screen before setting it down again. "We met in college and fell madly in love, but we broke up a little over two years ago because my life had begun to spin out of control. It was a messy breakup."

"I'm sorry to hear that," I told her.

"It's okay. I've made peace with it as best I can. At the time, I'd felt like I had no other choice. My parents hadn't exactly approved of the relationship either, which made it complicated.

Not having their approval wasn't insurmountable, because at the end of the day, I know they want me to be happy more than anything, but it caused a lot of friction and stress. Ultimately, I couldn't handle living in that heightened state, so I called it quits. In doing so, I'm pretty sure I made the biggest mistake of my entire life, because I lost the man I truly loved."

"That sounds devastating."

"It was extremely painful. I'm pretty sure I left my heart with him that day. He was an incredible man—*is* incredible. We were planning a life together, and I called it off." She idly stroked the throw pillow next to her, her red nails fiddling with the corner. "I love my family, as I've stated already. They are generous souls who would do anything for me. At the time, I chose to make their lives, as well as mine, easier in a time of turmoil. I thought it was the right choice. Turns out I was wrong."

"That was nice of you. I'm not sure if I could do the same."

She shrugged. "I have a healthy respect for my parents, but that's not the only reason I did it. Matt and I had graduated from Boston University a year or so prior, and he was contemplating a move to the West Coast to work at a very reputable security firm. I wasn't ready to leave my friends and family. It caused friction between us, which, now that I look back on it, was likely just growing pains. During that time, my parents decided that they no longer wanted to live in the US and were in the process of making a big move back to Morocco. My father is a talented engineer and had come over on a work visa many years ago. He'd been working at the same company for thirty years, but they missed their family back home and wanted to spend their retirement in Morocco. So they decided to sell everything and move. It all happened at once, proceeding very quickly, and was very stressful."

"It sounds like it. I'm sorry they're living so far away."

"I am, too. I miss them a lot. They've been gone for over a year now. They, of course, wanted me to join them, but I'm an American. I was born here. My life is here. I've been to Morocco many times, and I absolutely love the culture and the people, it's vibrant and beautiful, but it's never felt like my home. As their parting wish, they encouraged me to accept the arrangement with Marco. They wanted to make sure I'd be taken care of when they were gone so they wouldn't have to worry as much, even though sometimes I believe that worrying is their favorite pastime." She grinned. "I'd broken up with Matt six months prior, and even though I was tentative about starting a new relationship, I felt ready to head down this new path." Her phone beeped again. She picked it up, made a face, and stood, immediately shrugging her coat on. "Oh no. I'm sorry. I have to go. My meeting just got moved up, and I'm going to be late. I guess I didn't realize how much I had to say or how long it would take. Can we meet for drinks later so I can tell you the rest? Time is *literally* of the essence."

"Sure," I said, walking her to the door. "Let me give you my phone number."

She handed me her phone, and I entered my number as we walked.

"Before you leave," I said, "what's your proposition? I'm sort of dying to hear it. And, just so you know, I'm totally willing to help. Whatever it takes. I'm a sucker for happy endings, especially when they might include my own."

"I appreciate that." She smiled as she belted her coat. "Basically, I'm going on a little road trip tomorrow morning and could use the company."

"You want me to join you on a road trip?" Not what I was expecting, but certainly not out of the realm of possibilities.

"I do. It's kind of a wacky idea, but I need a partner in crime. All my good friends live on the East Coast, and I can't exactly ask Marco to join me, as it pertains to Matt, and that would be weird. I haven't told anybody at my job about my marriage arrangement and subsequent breakup with Marco, so it would be a little awkward to ask one of them to come with me. The problem is, I have to do it this weekend, or the window of opportunity might close for good. Matt is changing jobs next week, and getting him the note in person is important—if not critical. I'll pay for all the gas, and I have the accommodations lined up, thanks to a brilliant friend of mine. It should take two days at the most to get down there and back. Hopefully, a very quick trip."

"Where are we going?" At this point, I was pretty much all in.

"Montecito, California."

"What's in Montecito?"

"Prince Harry and Meghan Markle."

"Shut *uuuuuuuup!*" Poppy squealed. "Yasmine's ex-boyfriend is a bodyguard for the Duke and Duchess of Sussex?"

I glanced around the restaurant. "*Shhh.* Keep your voice down. She told me this in semiconfidence. I don't think she cares if I share it with you guys, but she doesn't want the world knowing." Or maybe she didn't care. It just seemed like something we should keep quiet. Poppy didn't do anything softly.

Poppy, Summer, and I sat in a booth at the Egg Shop, a brunch spot in Capitol Hill. I'd called them immediately after Yasmine had left. We'd met as soon as Poppy had been done with her meeting with Leo.

I hadn't shared any details until right this minute.

"That is *so* crazy." Summer shook her head. "What are the chances?"

"Yasmine was in a rush to get to work, so I got very few details out of her after that. But she has to deliver a note to Matt in person. Apparently, their mutual friends won't divulge his number, even though one of them has it on good authority that he's still in love with her. I don't know if they don't have it, or if they can't give it out because he's got this high-profile bodyguard job. But I know secrecy is involved."

"This is like a whodunit mystery," Poppy gushed. "Or who's going to *do* it." She waggled her eyebrows. "I love a spicy puzzle."

I reached for my cup of tea. "Yasmine realized, after Marco proposed, that settling for less than being absolutely in love is not acceptable for either of them. But it's not going to be easy to tell their parents that the marriage is off. They made it official, and now everyone expects them to move forward and get married."

"Except he's in love with you, and she's in love with Matt." Summer pointed her fork at me before using it to spear a chunk of omelet on her plate.

"'Love' is a strong word," I said. "Yasmine could definitely still be in love with Matt. And even though I've been infatuated with Marco for all these years, I have no idea what it'll be like to be together as a couple." But the possibilities were running through my mind nonstop.

We're going to have a chance to be together!

Huzzah!

"From what you've explained about your past multiyear infatuation with Marco"—Summer appeared thoughtful as she picked up her latte—"there might be some love involved."

"Maybe," I admitted.

When we first arrived at the restaurant, I'd quickly paraphrased for Summer everything I'd told Poppy last night about Marco. She'd taken it in stride and hadn't been as surprised as I'd thought she'd be.

She'd seen Marco and me with our heads together at the Driftwood, and she'd remembered me crushing on him almost eight years ago when the four of us had been living together in the dorms. She'd voiced her concerns to me then about getting too close to my old crush, which I'd denied would ever happen.

She'd been completely right.

"Never mind all that," Poppy said eagerly, waving her hand. "When are we leaving?"

"We?'" I set my teacup down.

"Damn right," Poppy stated. "I'll even donate the use of my car, since you said Yasmine's planning to rent something, and that would save her a chunk of change, but that means my body will be sitting inside of it." She tapped her index finger on the table. "If you think for even a sliver of a stinky little second that I'm missing out on seeing even a corner of Harry and Meghan's Montecito mansion, or getting a glimpse of their cute chicken coop, or seeing the little jungle gym where Archie and Lili play, then you haven't met me. I'm the biggest Anglophile in the entire world." She threw both her hands in the air with her standard dramatic flair. "I *live* for this crap. Just breathing the same air as them will be a gift." She waved her arms around, emulating air wafting in front of her face, turning her nose back and forth, sniffing.

I laughed. Summer laughed. How could we not?

"I wish I could go," Summer lamented. "But Xander has something special lined up for Saturday. We're driving up to Vancouver for the day. He has all this cute stuff planned he wants to do. The man is beyond adorable."

Poppy arched a brow in Summer's direction. "Your plate is literally running over with Mr. Raw Sexy. You can come next time." She glanced at me hopefully. "If there's a next time. There should be. And a time after that. Then maybe another one down the road. There'll never be enough times to see royalty. We could go literally every weekend and that would be fine with me."

I chuckled. "I don't have the authority to invite you to come along. This is not my plan. I was asked to accompany Yasmine. She did not ask me to ask all of my friends to join us."

"This is not *all* your friends," Poppy replied in a patient tone. "It's me, and possibly Annabel—because my sister lives for drama—you, Yasmine, and that's it. Four seats, four passengers. It's a perfect fit. We couldn't add anyone else anyway, which works out because Jenny has her residency, and Summer is busy with the Duke of Sexikins." Our friend Jenny was married to Daniel, and they had the cutest daughter, Clara. Jenny was on her way to becoming an orthopedic surgeon and had very little free time, but she would absolutely be sad to miss out on this. She wasn't as big an Anglophile as Poppy, but I knew she kept up with British royalty.

Summer chortled. "The Duke of Sexikins. That's hilarious. He's going to hate it, but I'm going to start using it. By the way"—she leaned forward, giving us a dramatic pause—"we're in discussions about whether or not he should move in."

I gasped.

Poppy clapped.

"That's amazing news," I said. "You and Xander are such a great match. I knew it would only be a matter of time before you moved in together." I was genuinely excited for my friend. She had dated a lot of duds before she'd found her match. When they were together, no one else existed. Their chemistry was off the charts.

"I'm so happy," she confided. "I love having him around. But I'm a little nervous that maybe it's too soon. My place is small, and there's nowhere to go if we get into an argument. Plus, it's not like I have space for his things. My own stuff is crammed in there like Jenga pieces. I'm not sure what we're going to do, but we're definitely negotiating." She grinned. "I should say, he's negotiating *hard*."

"Oh man, you guys are so juicy." Poppy giggled. "That's so fun. I'm incredibly happy for you. Moving in together is a big step. But we need to redirect back to the topic at hand, because we're running out of time." She pursed her lips and tilted her head, informing us she had a plan. "This road trip is set to begin in T-minus"—she picked up her phone and began tapping the screen—"eighteen hours. We should leave by at least six a.m. Seven at the latest. It takes sixteen hours to get there, so that means we'd arrive before midnight, which works—"

I sputtered, cutting her off. "How in the world do you know

how many hours it takes to get to Montecito?"

"*Aheeem*, weren't you listening?" She gave me a look accompanied by an expertly drawn eyebrow. "This is not my first rodeo. In fact, I've contemplated driving down there myself just to see the neighborhood up close and personal. This is going to be an absolute dream come true! I can hardly wait."

I didn't want to burst Poppy's bubble just yet, but I definitely needed to curtail her expectations. "Even if I get permission from Yasmine to have you join us," I told her, "this is all about *her* and what she needs to do. Not you and what you need to see."

I could actually envision Yasmine and Poppy being kindred spirits. Poppy was definitely going to love Yasmine, and Yasmine would have a hard time not enjoying Poppy. They just seemed like they'd get along well together.

"It's going to be all about her," Poppy declared. "I promise. Cross my heart." She traced an X over her chest with her finger. "Where are we staying, by the way?"

"She didn't give specifics. She was running out the door. She said only that she had it covered. We're going to meet tonight for drinks and iron out the details."

"Do you think Marco will be there?" Summer asked.

I shook my head. "I don't think so. Yasmine didn't mention it. I'm not sure if I'm ready to see him yet, to tell you the truth. Helping Yasmine first is important to me. Then he and I can come after that. I'll feel more settled that way. I'm still mortified that she knows we kissed last night. Even though she said it was fine, and they'd already broken up, I can't help feeling weird about it. It was such an impulsive thing to do. I really could've hurt her if she was in love with Marco."

Summer set her water glass on the table. "I don't think

Marco could be capable of doing something terrible to another human being. He's just not that type of guy."

"Does Marco know Yasmine came to visit you this morning?" Poppy asked. "This is quite a tangled web when you think about it."

It kind of was. "I didn't ask, but I'm assuming…yes? It seems like they share a lot. I'll ask her tonight."

Poppy set her napkin down and began to slide out of the booth. "This has been fun and all, but I've got to run. So many things to do and shore up before we leave." She was grinning so hard it was impossible not to giggle. "I'm going to have to write down instructions for Leo. The painters are coming by the brewpub this weekend. He'll just have to handle it." As she slid on her raincoat, she muttered, "I wish he wasn't acting so weird. That would make things a whole lot easier."

"Weird, how?" I asked.

"What you mean?" Summer asked.

"I don't know." Poppy sighed. "He's been completely distracted recently. Always looking at his phone, totally preoccupied. It's a little off-putting, but I'm dealing. Okay, enough about that. Text me when you get done speaking to Yasmine." She inclined her head at me. "I'll head out to get snacks after a talk with Leo." She was practically bouncing on the balls of her feet. "Then I'm going home to pack. I wonder if I should bring my sexy red dress with the scoop neck and the pleated skirt. It has a Marilyn Monroe vibe. Just in case Harry is out on the balcony, or something like that." She swished her hand. "Not that he would notice me, because Meghan is so blindingly beautiful, but what a story that would be!" She turned and hurried out of the restaurant, muttering, "Little red dress don't fail me now."

Both Summer and I were in stitches.

"She's not going to be deterred," Summer told me knowingly. "She's one thousand percent accompanying you to Montecito."

"I know," I said. "I'll have to find a way to break it to Yasmine tonight."

"I have a feeling Yasmine won't mind. She'll probably appreciate the company. From what you've told us about her, she seems super kind and is likely missing her own girlfriends. I'm sure they would've gone with her to track down Matt without a second thought."

"That's my guess, too."

"So, when do you and Marco finally get to go on a real date?" Summer asked, giving me a knowing look.

Date was code for finally hooking up with the man in my dreams.

I shrugged, trying not to feel completely overwhelmed by the idea. I picked up my tea. "I don't know. Probably once we get back from Montecito."

And hopefully not a single second later.

CHAPTER 5

You have to calm down," I warned Poppy. "Yasmine is going to think I brought a crazy lady with me."

We were parked in front of Marco's building, which was basically on Elliott Bay. It was super nice and modern. I'd never been inside, but I'd looked at plenty of real estate listings when they came up.

That's what people did when they're Obsessed.

But in a totally normal curious kind of way. Not stalkerish at all.

No, siree. Nothing to see here.

Yasmine and I had had drinks the night before and formulated a loose plan. I hadn't shared everything with Poppy yet because I knew she would low-key lose her mind when she found out the details.

"I really think I should drive," Annabel suggested to Poppy from the back seat. "The way you're acting, having a stroke is not out of the realm of possibilities."

Poppy whipped her head around. "I'm not going to have a stroke! I'm just gleefully excited. This is what gleeful looks like. You should try it sometime. And, news flash, it can happen without physical injury."

"Here comes Yasmine," I said, opening the passenger door and stepping out. She carried a small duffel and a large purse. She was dressed in yoga pants and a tangerine-colored T-shirt, still managing to look glamorous. "Hello," I called, giving her a wave.

"Hey." She waved back. "Thank you so much for doing this. Marco is actually right inside. He'd like to talk to you, if that's okay?"

My eyebrows hit my hairline. "Right now? He wants to talk *now*?" It was six thirty in the morning, and we hadn't stopped for coffee yet. The last time I'd seen Marco, we'd been sucking pony tongue in the closet. I'd told my friends yesterday I wasn't ready to see him, and I'd meant it. I wanted to help Yasmine, then settle into my new reality with Marco. Honestly, now that I knew everything that had gone on between Yasmine and Marco, I felt embarrassed that he and I had lost control.

"Yep, now would be good," Yasmine answered.

Poppy hopped out of the driver's side, buzzing around to the trunk, popping it open. "Hi," she chirped to Yasmine more exuberantly than necessary for this time of the morning. "We met briefly the other night. Thank you for allowing us to accompany you on your mission. This is going to be so fun!"

Yasmine chuckled. "Mission? I like the sound of that. It *is* kind of a mission." She set her bag inside the trunk, keeping her purse with her. "And I'm happy that you wanted to join us. The more the merrier."

"My sister, Annabel, is in the back seat," Poppy said. "I'll introduce you to her while Eve goes to talk to Marco." Poppy motioned me forward with a flick of her wrist. "Go, go. We have a schedule to keep."

"Fine," I grumbled, butterflies instantly attacking my stomach and fluttering up my esophagus.

As I moved toward the front of the building, Marco came out. He wore brown slippers, blue and green plaid pajama pants, and a white T-shirt and held a navy mug that most likely had coffee in it.

One of us had gotten a jump on the day.

The man was stunning.

I began to salivate.

His black hair was slightly mussed, and his biceps flexed as he brought the cup to his lips.

As casually as I could, I brought my shirtsleeve up and wiped my lips.

Good grief, I had to get a grip.

"Hi," he said shyly.

I was feeling equally as shy. "Hi. It's, um, nice to see you."

"You, too." He raked a hand through his hair. It stuck up every which way. I was mesmerized. I wanted to touch it. I wanted to rub my face in it. This was getting out of hand. "Listen, I'm really sorry I didn't explain the arrangement I had with Yasmine and everything that's been going on. It's just… it's taken us some time to figure everything out—"

"It's not a problem at all," I cut in. I didn't feel like this was the time or place to have this conversation. Especially when I wanted to lap my pony tongue all over his body. "You didn't owe me any explanations. Your business is yours."

He chuckled. It was a wonderful sound. "It was my business until I brought you into the closet with me. Then it became our business, and I should've explained myself. If not immediately, I should've texted or called you as soon as possible. I was just"—he rubbed the back of his neck, his biceps popping—"overwhelmed, I think. But I don't regret kissing you at all. Yasmine knows about my feelings. I just didn't know how to explain everything to you in that moment. The champagne didn't help. Or maybe it helped too much. Hard to know."

I'd zoned out a little after he said *our business.*

Us. Two people together. A couple.

"Don't worry." I hoped my voice sounded casual. "Yasmine told me everything."

"I'm glad somebody knows what's going on." He chuckled good-naturedly. "She's being a little tightlipped about what's happening this weekend, but I know she's really excited. I'm guessing it has something to do with Matt."

I smiled, not knowing what to say. Yasmine would've told him what she wanted him to know. "It might be."

He shuffled his feet. "When you get back, I'm hoping we can…you know…get together and go on an actual date."

He was nervous.

It was endearing.

In this moment, I could absolutely understand why it took him and Yasmine more than a year to figure out that their relationship wasn't going to work. He was just so amicable and sweet. It was clear he didn't want to hurt anyone's feelings. He was definitely a guy who wouldn't do something hurtful on purpose.

"We can. Definitely." I stared at his lips, even though I was trying not to, remembering how soft and perfect and kissable they were. "That would be great. So nice." When he didn't reply readily, I continued like a babbling brook that couldn't be stopped come hell or high water. "Next time, we'll keep the champagne out of it." We'd both imbibed that night. The alcohol, along with the adrenaline of having the business-christening party together, had been a heady mix. *Too* heady.

Thinking back, it'd been kind of animalistic what we'd done. Like we couldn't breathe for one more single second without touching or tasting each other. Going without physical contact at the time had seemed impossible. And sneaking off together had been so contrary to both our characters, it had to have been some kind of uncontrollable impulse.

As I stood in front of him, watching him flex his beautiful biceps as he drank his coffee, I felt that urge rise again.

My fingers curled as I imagined his hard chest beneath them, of tasting his soft lips again, at having another chance to be lost in his methodical kisses. I wanted to smell him and stroke his face. I wanted to lave him from head to toe. My tongue flicked around inside my mouth as I imagined how he would taste.

I want this man with everything I have!

I felt a little itchy all of a sudden. "I should probably get going." Had that come out as a croak? It had felt like a croak. "They're waiting." I gestured behind me without looking, my eyes still locked on the prize.

"You have my number," he said. "Text me and let me know what's happening."

"Will do," I said, taking a few steps backward.

Why was this so awkward?

Maybe because his fiancée was sitting in a car, waiting for me. Or we were both just nerdy introverts.

"I'll check in at the shop while you're gone," he told me.

"Thanks. No deliveries are scheduled until next Wednesday." We'd just assumed the lease a week prior. There were a million things to do, but they could wait for two days. My Excel spreadsheet prowess was on point. My day job was as an accountant after all. "We've got that handyman interview on Monday," I reminded him. "See you then."

He winked. "Unless I see you first."

Oh my goodness, this man is so hooooot.

I turned and bolted for the car, trying to do my best sexy run. Because he was probably looking at my butt, right? I would definitely be looking at his if our positions were reversed. Eyes in the back of my head would be so helpful at times like these.

Yasmine was in the back seat next to Annabel. I leaned through the open door. "You're welcome to sit up front," I told her.

"I'm fine back here."

I got in the passenger seat and buckled up.

"Thank you all so much for coming with me," Yasmine said. "It's kind of weird to go on a road trip with people I hardly know, but I think it'll be fun. At least I hope it will be."

"It's not weird at all. And it'll totally be fun." Poppy put the car in reverse and backed out of the parking spot. "And it's us who need to thank *you*. Getting within sniffing distance of the Duke and Duchess of Sussex will be a real treat. Plus, we're all here to help facilitate happy endings. It's kind of what we live for."

"I don't want to disappoint you," Yasmine cautioned. "I have no idea if Meghan and Harry are home. I actually know nothing about them, only that they've hired great security."

"Seeing them would be marvelous, of course," Poppy replied nonchalantly. "But honestly, just being able to see their setup in person would be enough. If they actually tried to talk to me, I would likely lose my mind, anyway. So this is much better in the end."

"She would actually lose her mind. I'm here to verify," Annabel confirmed. "Like, it would be gone. Zippo. Only mush left. I've seen it happen a few times. It's not pretty. She turns into an actual Muppet." Annabel held up her hand and mimicked a talking sock puppet. "No sound comes out. She stands there googly-eyed and glazed over."

"Way to paint the picture, Bell," Poppy said, making a silly face at her sister in the rearview mirror. "I've only done that, like, twice. Once when I ran into Pierce Brosnan on the beach. I mean, have you seen those crystal-blue eyes up close and personal? To *die* for. It was an out-of-body experience. A superb chef's kiss. And the other was"—she snapped her fingers twice—"what's her name? She was one of the original judges on *American Idol.*"

"Paula Abdul?" I suggested.

"No." Poppy was still snapping. "This woman was only on for a couple of seasons. Kind of in the beginning? Maybe season seven or eight? Hard to remember."

"Are you sure she's not fictitious?" Annabel snarked. "You could've made her up, like an imaginary friend. That's happened before."

"Hardy, har, *har.* You know who I'm talking about. You watched it with me. She had long, dark hair. She was there with

Randy and Simon. I think she replaced Paula. I kind of remember an uproar about it. She was a super-talented songwriter who wrote hundreds of songs. She cowrote 'Walk Away' by Kelly Clarkson. I was *obsessed* with that song and her."

"I think her name was Kara something," Yasmine offered. "*American Idol* was a staple in our house. I never missed an episode."

"That's it!" Poppy cried. "Kara DioGuardi. She was my absolute favorite. I never missed an episode either. I *idolized* that show. Pun intended."

"She can't be your absolute favorite when you can't even remember her name," Annabel quipped.

"I was, like, twelve when I met her," Poppy said. "The second season she was on, Mom took me to a local mall where the show was scouting talent, because as previously stated, I was obsessed. And she was there. She came up to us and said hi. It was the first time my mouth didn't work properly. I couldn't say a word. Zero sound came out. I felt like I was in the middle of a fever dream. And I'd brought something to give her, too. A sweaty piece of paper was tucked in my pocket. I'd written a song, but I was too frozen in place to grab it. One of my top-ten regrets in life. But that's it, I swear." She put one palm across her heart. "No other celebrity zombie instances."

"I'm so curious. What was the song?" I asked. "And, by the way, that's completely adorable. I can totally picture you waiting for your big opportunity and then being totally starstruck."

"I can only remember the first part." Poppy tapped her fingers against the steering wheel for a beat. Her head began to bob back and forth as she sang, "I went downtown to see the people, the people were gathered around. I looked for my baby in every store, but my baby just wasn't round." She began to laugh. "It was such a corny country vibe, but I thought I was the shit for coming up with it. I was convinced it would hit the top of the charts if anyone decided to record it. No music, mind you. Just the lyrics. And I couldn't even get it out of my pocket to give it to my favorite idol, because there was nothing floating around in my brain but air."

Annabel chuckled. "If Kara DioGuardi can render you speechless, you might be in danger of spontaneously combusting if Prince Harry were to actually look you dead in the eye."

"I mean, probably not, because self-combustion is rare," Poppy argued. "But if that *did* happen, and the ginger prince sent his hauntingly beautiful gaze my way, I'd likely be in need of resuscitation. So I hope everyone is up to date on their CPR certification. By the way, I like my lifesaving breaths of air with a little tongue. It makes things more interesting."

We giggled.

"I'm sorry to burst your bubble," I said, still chortling, "but it's very unlikely that we're *actually* going to see royalty. In its essence, this is a stealth mission. All we need to do is make our way to the perimeter of their house and flag down one of the bodyguards." At least that's how I understood it.

"Is that the actual plan?" Annabel asked. "Because getting to the perimeter could be tricky. Meghan and Harry likely live in a gated community, or at the very least, their property is gated. I'm not sure how we're going to get through the gate, much less get close enough to deliver the intended offerings."

Poppy made a gurgling noise. "If you're such a Negative Nellie, why did you come with us? We're totally fulfilling this mission! We're breaching that perimeter if it's the last thing we do."

"No negativity here, I swear," Annabel said. "Just being real. And did you actually think I'd stay home and miss witnessing you try to breach any perimeter—much less the Duke and Duchess of Sussex's? I know the depth of your determination. You're not above covering yourself in honey and leaves to blend in, buzz-cutting your hair, snapping off a lock with your teeth, or enlisting nearby schoolchildren to get the job done, uncaring of any consequences."

"Damn straight," Poppy said. "We are getting the special message to…"

"Matt Gallagher," Yasmine helpfully supplied, seeming amused.

"…Matt Gallagher if it kills us," Poppy concluded. "That man is getting *served*."

I chuckled. "Hmmm. Nobody here is willing to risk bodily harm, so maybe let's not do anything related to dying. Just, like, we will get him the letter over our moderately steadfast bodies."

"No one is hurting themselves." Yasmine backed me up. "And just so you all feel better, we're staying in the house right next door. My friend didn't know for sure, but she thinks only hedges separate the properties. So it should be fairly easy to flag someone down on the other side."

"We're *what?*" Poppy croaked from the driver seat, her head whipping around, mouth gaping.

My hand hovered near the steering wheel in case I needed to intervene.

"Next door? *Really?*" Annabel sounded equally as shocked.

"Really," Yasmine confirmed.

I braced myself, knowing that Poppy would likely have some sort of frantic hyper anxiety attack at the next bit, which was why

I hadn't told her all the specifics yet.

"You know," I said before Yasmine could explain further, "I think it'd be better if we pull over and get our coffee for the road before you tell them the rest. I'd love for this to happen when Poppy is *not* behind the wheel."

"That sounds like a plan." Yasmine laughed. "I had no idea you loved the royal family so much, Poppy. I should've come to you a few weeks ago."

"You should have!" Poppy said as she merged onto an off-ramp. "Are you kidding? The greatest regret of my entire life was not being born in time to see Princess Diana get married. I've watched that footage so many times, but it's not the same. I cried for ten hours straight when Kate and William tied the knot. Meghan and Harry about did me in. I used to ask Santa to make me British every year until I was about nine years old. I'd wake up on Christmas morning hoping he'd blessed me with a cockney accent. True story."

Annabel giggled. "And even though Santa didn't grant that particular wish, you woke up with an accent anyway. You'd come down with a cheerful 'cheerio' and proceed to speak in a mangled British accent for the next few hours. It was annoying, but if I'm being honest, it was also completely adorable."

"Of course it was adorable! And I'm never annoying. Take it back." Poppy took a right and then pulled into the parking lot of a coffee shop that was part of a Seattle chain. "The accent always wore off much too soon. Once I began opening all my exciting toys, I became distracted. But there was always next year." She smiled at Yasmine in the rearview mirror. "Once I take this key out of this ignition, you're going to need to spill all the juicy details, because I'm about to pee my pants in anticipation."

Chapter 6

"*Oh my God. Oh my God*," Poppy chanted as she paced back and forth next to the car, fanning herself with her hands, then shaking them out beside her like she'd lost feeling in both of her arms. "Your friend's parents *own* the literal house next door? A fifty-two-million-dollar megamansion? Are you kidding me? And we're going to *sleep* there?"

"How in the world do you know how much it costs?" I asked.

Poppy snapped her head toward me, peering at me through narrowed eyes. "Did you not hear everything I just said in the car?" She whipped one of her arms around like a fan blade. "I follow it all. The house next door was previously owned by Rob Lowe. He sold it not too long ago, then it just sold again. It's a colonial mansion, and it's *breath-tak-ing-ly* beautiful. Not only have I seen the photos on the Zillow listing, but I've also searched for the aerial photos. This is so epic! I don't know what to do." She turned in a circle and began to mutter to herself. "I'm staying at Rob Lowe's house. I'm staying in his mansion. How did this happen?"

Annabel came to the rescue, gently gripping her sister by the shoulders and guiding her toward the coffee shop as we began to walk. "Just put one foot in front of the other, and you'll be fine," Annabel soothed. "It's all going to be okay."

"You can play low-key all you want, but I know you," Poppy piped over her shoulder at Annabel. "There's no way that this is *not* affecting you. You can act like you're too cool for school, but you're freaking out inside just like me. You might not be an Anglophile, but you went through a primo Goth retro childhood phase. There was many a late night that you spent pining over *St. Elmo's Fire* and *The Breakfast Club* wishing like hell you'd been alive in the eighties. As much as I wanted to be British, you wanted to be Molly Ringwald."

"I wanted to *date* Molly Ringwald," Annabel corrected, her mouth quirking. "There's a difference."

"Ha. Keep telling yourself that." We entered the small shop and got in line. "You were just as affected by the cuteness of young Rob Lowe as I was. You crush on both men and women, so don't lie. And we're going to his house! We're going to touch things he touched! Like the cupboards and the faucets and…and the doorknobs."

Annabel giggled. "You're going to stroke the cupboards, aren't you?"

"Of course," Poppy stated with certainty. "And the countertops and maybe the bathtub."

"Okay, the bathtub just makes it creepy." Annabel made a face.

"You're right. Instead of stroking it, I'll just take an actual bath." Poppy snickered. "Then I can swish my whole body around." She did a few hip curls while waving her arms.

"Unfortunately," I said, "new owners who are that wealthy probably update the everyday stuff." I mean, I didn't know that many millionaires, but that sounded correct.

"There are pictures," Poppy said. "We can cross-reference. That way, I'll know exactly what's new and what's old."

Yasmine seemed to be taking all the banter in stride, grinning as she ordered her latte.

Once everybody had their coffee, we made our way back outside.

Back in the car, Poppy announced, "Okay, new plan. We're gunning it all the way there without stopping. Sixteen hours in one go." She held up a single finger. "Before our final destination was announced, I thought maybe we'd do it more leisurely, but that's not the case anymore, so be prepared to pee in a can. This bus is not stopping."

"Nobody's peeing in a can," I corrected. "We don't even have one. Plus, you have to stop and get gas along the way."

Poppy pulled out of the parking lot, shaking her head. "If you have to pee before we need gas, we're not stopping. I have a ton of snacks packed, including several water bottles. That'll get us through the day. If we need potty receptacles, we have them."

I chuckled. "I know you're not being serious. There's no way we're peeing in a bottle."

"My car, my rules." She pulled out onto the street.

"This burger is *sooo* good," Poppy moaned around her first bite. "I thought I might die of starvation."

"Starvation was your plan, not ours," Annabel said as she bit into her patty melt.

We were in a booth at a roadside diner outside Redding, California, which was a little over halfway to Montecito. We'd been in the car a full nine hours.

"Yum, you're right," Annabel said. "This is excellent. Super soaked with grease, just the way I like it."

"Your snacks were delicious," I told Poppy as I took a bite of my own burger. "But an apple, a granola bar, and a handful of dried apricots do not a meal make."

"Okay," Poppy said around another mouthful, "I admit not stopping to eat was an unrealistic goal, but we've made great time, so hitting up this burger joint was indeed a good choice."

"It was the only choice if you didn't want us to gnaw off our arms," Annabel stated. "Which would've derailed the mission and messed up your car." She took another bite, and her eyes rolled back in her head.

I glanced at Yasmine, who sat next to me. She was looking at her phone. "Has Kelly replied yet?" Kelly was the friend of a friend who was allowing us to stay in her parents' multimillion-dollar mansion. Apparently, Kelly's parents were vacationing in the South of France, as the rich did, and she'd said they wouldn't mind.

Our plan moving forward hadn't been locked into place yet, but I wasn't going to worry about it. Okay, so I was, because my anxiety wouldn't let me off scot-free, but I knew we'd figure things out before we got there. We had seven hours left on the road.

Plenty of time.

"She hasn't," Yasmine said, popping a fry into her mouth. "But Marley, my friend who connected us, said she's probably working late. Kelly works at Goop, and apparently Gwyneth Paltrow makes them work long hours. Or maybe it's weird hours? I can't remember." Yasmine shrugged as she picked up another fry. "I was in touch with her two days ago. She gave me the address and told me where we could sleep. Apparently, there are quite a few guest rooms, but we still need the gate codes."

"The infamous gate codes," Annabel snarked. "See?" She nodded toward her sister. "I was right. Without them, you wouldn't be able to honey-camo your way in."

"Eh," Poppy replied. "I'd find a way."

"Once Kelly gets back to you, have her confirm whether or not she let the staff know we're arriving," I said. "A house that big, they have to have staff, right?"

Anxiety. It was an ever-existing presence. I'd named mine Ophelia sometime in high school after reading *Hamlet*. Equating my inner struggle to Ophelia's tragic story just seemed right.

"Kelly told me the house would be empty," Yasmine said. "But I'll double-check. She also said to absolutely not approach Meghan and Harry's front gate. She advised that we go through the yard. They monitor the gate with cameras and just yell through the speaker at strangers to get lost."

"They must have a lot of people coming to check it out," I said.

"This is so freaking exciting." Poppy finished the last of her burger, clapping the crumbs off of her fingers. "We've gone over some scenarios, but Yasmine doesn't know which shift Matt is on, so we can do the deed right when we get there at midnight or wait until morning. What do you guys think?"

"What exactly are we delivering, again?" Annabel asked Yasmine. "You said it was a letter, but also something personal."

Yasmine furrowed her brows for a brief moment as a small blush crept along her cheeks. "Yes, a letter. Our breakup was a little rocky, so I had a lot to say about the way I handled things. Along with the letter, I'm delivering a pocketknife."

"We're smuggling a *weapon* across the border?" Poppy's face morphed to incredulous.

"What border are you talking about?" I chuckled. "The hedge border? You realize that we're not actually crossing into the UK, right?"

"It's not a weapon," Yasmine answered. "Okay, so technically it *is*, but it's not. It's something really important to Matt. His dad was in the Air Force, and he picked it up on his travels and gave it to Matt when he turned twelve. Matt lost it about a month or two before we broke up. I found it while I was packing up to move to Seattle. I tried to get a hold of him then, but had no luck. He's not on social media, and my friends didn't have his new number. He'd already moved to California by that time. When he sees it, he's going to be so relieved and excited. Honestly, if giving that back to him is the only thing I accomplish on this trip, at least I did something right."

"It won't be the only thing you accomplish," I reassured her. "He's going to see your letter, and he's going to have feelings about it."

Yasmine shook her head. "I'm not so sure he will. The more we drive, the more hesitant I am that I'm doing the right thing. I have no idea if he's in a relationship with someone else or not. I have no clue if he still has feelings for me. This could blow up in my face."

"I don't think it will," I told her.

She picked up her soda. "I can't help but feel that I've built this up in my head to be some sort of happy ending for myself that might be impossible to achieve. My family might have a hard time that Marco and I are breaking up, but they'll get over it eventually. I don't need to have somebody waiting in the wings." She took a sip through her paper straw. "Maybe we should just go back to Seattle."

"No." I reached out to touch her arm. "We should definitely see this through. Whatever the situation is with Matt, he's going to get a chance to read your true feelings. From what you told me last night and what you've shared with us in the car over the last nine hours, there was a deep love between you. That doesn't just evaporate into thin air. If anything, this will be cathartic for both of you. Then you can clear the slate and move forward, knowing you did all you could with no regrets."

"Eve's right," Annabel said. "If he was as brokenhearted as you described about the breakup and recently confided in the friend that he still has feelings for you, he's going to be really excited about this. This is exactly what you need to do."

"They're both right," Poppy agreed. "You haven't shared everything, but you've shared enough that we've all gotten a vivid picture of what it was like when you and Matt were together, how happy you were, the sacrifice you made for your family, your journey with Marco, and your decision to marry for true love. You've had that kind of love once, and you can have it again. There is no reason on this earth to settle for less than that. Getting Matt that letter is essential. And even if he doesn't turn out to be your true love, there is a guy out there somewhere who will be." Poppy glanced around the table. "Speaking of delivering the letter, do we think any old bodyguard will deliver it and the pocketknife to Matt? Or do we have to, like, ask them for their credentials? Or at least find out if they know each other first?"

"Asking if they know him would probably be a good idea," I said. "We want to be sure the letter and pocketknife get to him." We were almost done with our meal. I'd enjoyed every last bite of my burger and fries. They were delicious. There was nothing like a roadside diner with its shiny metal counter, checkered stools, and red pleather booths. I wished I'd ordered a malt, particularly as I watched Annabel happily slurping hers. "But overall, I think whoever we end up talking to will be civil. It's not like they're going to go full SWAT on us if we approach. We can just pretend we're Kelly's friends, hanging out and having a good time, and we just 'happened'"—air quotes around *happened*—"to come too close to the property line."

Annabel giggled. "Oh, and by the way, we have some specific things for you to deliver to your coworker. What a coincidence!"

"We can pretend we were hiking and lost our sense of direction," Poppy said. "I mean, those properties are gigantic."

I raised an eyebrow her way. "I'm not sure you know what 'hiking' means. You can't *hike* in a yard."

"You can, too, if it's hilly," she argued.

I laughed. "Regardless, we're on the adjacent property with permission. Getting a note to a fellow bodyguard sounds pretty benign to me. They'll probably think it's cute."

"You haven't seen royal bodyguards," Poppy said. "They hardly ever crack a smile."

"They're not supposed to smile," I replied. "If they went

around looking happy all day, they wouldn't seem very fearsome. But I'm sure when they're by themselves, they joke around, and it's not so intense."

"It's intense when they're in an active situation," Yasmine said. "Matt graduated with a degree in criminology. He's always been fascinated by crime, but he's so big, he landed a job as a bouncer his freshman year in college. He was so well-liked at that bar, some guy who does private security hired him his senior year to accompany Matt Damon around every time he came to Boston, which is where he's from, so he visited a lot."

"You met Matt Damon?" Poppy's mouth could not have tumbled open any farther. She could have fit a whole burger in there.

"Only once," Yasmine admitted. "He was super nice. Just how you'd imagine he'd be. He was gracious and charming. I didn't make it a habit to accompany my Matt on his jobs, though, so it was only the one time."

"That's incredibly cool," I said.

"Because the money was so good," Yasmine continued, "Matt debated switching career paths and becoming a bodyguard full-time. It was one of the things we argued about. He wanted to move to California because he'd been offered a position at this high-brow security firm right out of college. But I wanted him to stay and pursue his love of criminology and all that that entailed. Plus, I really wanted to live on the East Coast. It's where my family was before they moved back to Morocco. It's where all my friends are. But here I am, living on the West Coast. Just not with him. The world is funny sometimes."

"You said this was your last chance to deliver your note and knife because Matt is changing jobs. What's he doing next?"

Poppy asked.

"I have no idea," Yasmine said. "Only that he'll no longer be with his current security firm. That's all the information my friend could give me. I'm really hoping he found a job in his field. That would make me so happy."

Our waitress came and cleared our plates, leaving our tab.

"It's probably time to get back on the road," I said. "If we keep up the good time, we should arrive around midnight. We can decide what our plan should be once we get there."

Annabel set some money on the table. "I've got this one. This is a cash-only joint." Yasmine tried to add to the pile, and Annabel shook her head. "You've paid for all of the gas thus far. This is on me." She glanced at her sister. "You can pay me back later."

"Rude," Poppy grumbled as we scooted from the booth. "I'm the one who's doing all the driving, and I bought the snacks."

"The only reason you're driving," Annabel quipped. "is because you won't let anybody else take the wheel. And as a bonus, you can pay me back in umbrellas. I'm sadly short, and you have fifty thousand."

"How in the world did you think it was okay to move to Seattle without bringing an umbrella?" Poppy playfully scolded. "You can have the light blue one with the ducks on it as a burger deduction. One of the tines, or whatever they're called, is broken, but it still works." Once outside, she began to skip toward the car. "Hurry up! The duke and duchess await."

CHAPTER 7

"Are we in the right place?" Poppy's forehead was all but pressed up against the windshield as she peered out into the dark, the car's headlights illuminating the gate in front of us.

Yasmine sat in the passenger seat next to her. They put their heads together to read Kelly's last text.

It'd come in only an hour ago.

Better late than never.

"They're pretty cagey around here." Annabel yawned, stretching her arms and shifting to change her position in her seat. "The address was posted back by the street next to those three mailboxes. It's going to be hard to know which megamansion is the right one."

We'd turned up a side road that serviced three properties and had stopped in front of the first gate on the left.

"I'm pretty sure this is it," Yasmine said.

Poppy had her maps app open and was doing the Google

Earth thing.

Then she gasped.

"What?" I asked, craning my neck around to make sure police cars weren't rolling up. "Are we in the wrong place?"

"No. This is it," Poppy confirmed. "But right up there, just a few hundred feet, is the entrance to Harry and Meghan's property." She gestured with a flapping motion like the story was on the tip of her tongue, but she couldn't get it out because she was too verklempt. "We're so…*close*. They…they drive on this road. We are on the same road they drive on. Our tires have touched the same surface their tires have touched. Or maybe they walk the dog here, and their shoes have touched the same places. Oh my God, this is a Kevin Bacon six degrees thing. Nothing separates us but the gravel!" She covered her mouth with her hand.

Um, not exactly how that worked.

We let her have her moment.

When she was done, she dropped her hand and straightened her shoulders. "Okay. I'm back. Let's figure this out."

Annabel leaned into the front seat, peering at the gate. 'It doesn't look like there's a place to punch in a code or anything. It just looks like a speaker coming up out of the ground with a red button."

She was right.

In front of us, a large black gate blocked the entrance to a long driveway. It looked like the gate swung in only one direction. There didn't appear to be anywhere to enter a security code.

"Kelly said there's a remote behind one of the big rocks," Poppy said.

"A remote?" I asked.

"Yeah, they use it for staff and delivery people when they're out of town, or something like that," Yasmine said. "We just have to find it, aim it at the gate, and it should open." She unbuckled her seat belt and opened her car door, getting out.

We all did the same, leaving the car idling with the headlights on.

I glanced over my shoulder, half expecting security guards to already be approaching because we were making so much noise. It was twelve twenty-five a.m., and even though we were trying to be quiet, I felt like we were being loud. I also felt like we were trespassing.

"Kelly said the remote is on the right, but there are a whole bunch of rocks here," Poppy said.

The four of us began to search for the hidden device.

After five minutes of constant searching, Poppy placed her hands on her hips. "I don't see it, and we've looked behind every single rock. Kelly's not answering Yasmine's texts or calls."

"That doesn't leave us with a lot of options," I said.

Annabel offered, "We can sleep in the car."

Poppy gaped at her sister like she'd uttered a string of filthy words. "We are *not* sleeping in the car! We've come all this way to see the inside of a fifty-two-million-dollar mansion that was once owned by a nineties heartthrob."

"Eighties," Annabel corrected. "He was an eighties heartthrob."

"He was still working in the nineties and still very cute. In fact, he really hasn't aged very much." Poppy contemplated that information with pursed lips.

"He could be a vampire," Annabel said. "That would make this situation infinitely more interesting."

"Yeah, but he doesn't live here anymore," I pointed out. 'So he's, like, hunting in a new place now."

"Very funny." Poppy gestured toward the gate. "We're getting in there. We just have to look harder."

Yasmine was on the other side, searching the rocks there. I joined her.

"Anything else come in from Kelly?" I asked.

"Nothing," she replied from behind a midsize rock. "I can't help but feel like she's ghosting me. My friend Marley said she's reliable and nice. But the remote is clearly not here. Maybe we're in the wrong place and we should find a motel for the night and come back in the morning."

I glanced at the end of the gate we were closest to. There was a gap between it and the hedge line. "Or we can leave the car here and slip through that gap and see if we're in the right place. If we're not, we can leave quietly. We're all small enough to make it through."

A grown man wouldn't fit, but I was betting we all could.

Yasmine glanced at the possible way in, then back at me. "Do you think we should?"

I shrugged. "Why not? We have permission from the daughter of the couple who owns this place to stay here. We're not breaking and entering. If we're at the wrong house, once we get there, we can just explain what happened."

"Breaking and entering where?" Annabel asked, walking up.

I gestured at the gap. "We can get through right there if we leave the car here."

"This Kelly girl told us to use the remote, not sneak in." Annabel broke out into a full grin. "But I'm all for it. We're all basically in a travel coma. We need to sleep, and life is nothing without a little adventure."

"I totally agree," Poppy said, joining us. "We can fill our pockets with snacks. Yasmine, grab your letter and pocketknife, and let's get in there. I'd bet my life we're at the right house. Excuse me, *mansion*."

"You and your snacks," Annabel muttered as we all walked back to the car.

"I'm making sure we all survive, which is more than I can say for you," Poppy said. "It's not like there's a fully staffed diner in there with juicy burgers and malts waiting for us."

"Eating their food would be weird," I said. "I'm happy to have the snacks."

We opened the car doors and retrieved our essentials. We wouldn't be able to fit luggage or duffels through the gap, but we could definitely take our purses, toothbrushes, and jammies.

It would have to do.

Poppy pulled the car closer to the gate before shutting it off.

Once she turned off the headlights, we were in the dark. Not a streetlight for miles.

One by one, we turned on the flashlights on our phones.

"Okay, who's going first?" I asked.

"Annabel," Poppy offered.

"I will," Yasmine said at the same time. "I dragged you all here in the first place. It's only right I should go first."

"Did you just offer me up as a sacrificial lamb?" Annabel asked her sister.

"Of course," Poppy replied, unfazed. "With your Amazonian strength, you'll be able to fight off the Dobermans that are probably patrolling the yard, giving us regular humans with short, stubby legs enough time to escape."

"A Doberman could fit through that gap," Annabel said knowingly. "But on the other hand, a Rottweiler might have a harder time."

I giggled. "Come on, you two, Yasmine's already halfway through."

We followed her through the gap.

It was a little tight, but it worked.

"Thank goodness none of us has big boobs," Annabel said as she squeezed through last. She was definitely the tallest of us. "Boobs would definitely be a dealbreaker in this scenario."

Once on the other side, we all crouched down.

"Why are we crouching?" I whispered.

"It seems appropriate," Poppy whispered back. "We have to see the lay of the land before we continue."

"Who knows what rich people could deploy in a response to intruders? There are clearly no dogs," Annabel said. "But they could have attack gerbils or a herd of geese waiting in the wings."

"Geese come in gaggles," Poppy replied matter-of-factly. "They're all honk and no game."

"Gerbils?" I questioned. "Why in the world did you pick gerbils?"

"Why not gerbils?" Annabel said. "They're totally feisty, and I bet, with enough money, you could link some sort of Habitrail from the house to here. If the gerbils were extra starving, they could come for faces." She mocked clawing at her eyes with curled fingers. "They could probably gnaw off a good portion of a nose before we could swat them away."

"Good grief," I said, laughing. "Your imagination knows no bounds, Annabel. I'm pretty sure homeowners wouldn't waste their money on attack gerbils. If they wanted to, they could just dig a moat and fill it with alligators."

"She did not get the brains in the family. Sorry, folks," Poppy chirped. "Follow me." She began to creep along the hedge line, staying off the actual paved driveway.

The driveway seemed to go on for a mile, but in reality, it was probably a block long. We finally edged around a corner to find a bigger paved parking area. A few lights were strategically placed in the plants to illuminate the front of the home. Everything else was dark.

"Oh my goodness, it looks like the White House," Poppy squealed in an awe-filled, reverent voice, placing a hand over her heart. "Look at those columns. All those black-framed windows. My dream home in a nutshell."

"That's an awfully big nut." Annabel guffawed.

The house was crazy enormous and really beautiful. You could tell how immaculate it was even in the low light. "I'm pretty sure I've never been this close to a house this big," I said.

"Honestly, human beings don't need this much space," Annabel said. "I watched a show once about super-efficient apartments in crazy-large cities abroad. People can do a lot with five hundred square feet. If you have the right gadgets, it can even seem spacious."

"Those people are not Rob Lowe," Poppy muttered, continuing forward.

"I don't see a lockbox or a place for a key code or anything like that," I said.

"Kelly said there's a service entrance farther down," Yasmine said. "Let's hope she's right."

We continued to walk along the house, staying in the driveway.

I was extremely thankful no alarms had gone off. It definitely felt like we were trespassing, even more so now. We were creeping around like Peeping Toms.

Inside my pants pocket, my phone chimed with Marco's sound.

I pulled it out, grinning already.

WHAT ARE YOU UP TO? ARE YOU THERE YET?

I stopped walking as more text bubbles came up.

I'VE BEEN THINKING ABOUT YOU. ABOUT US.

More bubbles.

I held my breath.

I CAN'T WAIT FOR YOU TO GET BACK.

I began to text my response as we walked, still searching for the service entrance, whatever that was.

I CAN'T WAIT TO BE BACK.

Then I texted:

WE ARE IN MONTECITO. BUT THINGS ARE A LITTLE FISHY. I'M NOT SURE WE'RE IN THE RIGHT PLACE.

He responded immediately.

SEND ME YOUR LOCATION.

I thought about it for half a second. It was a good idea. I whispered to the girls, "I'm sending Marco our location just in case something happens."

"What could possibly happen?" Poppy said a half second before a floodlight snapped on, and we all dived for the bushes.

After a few seconds, nothing else happened, and we all began to nervous-giggle.

"Okay, we have to get a grip," Annabel said as she stood, brushing herself off. We all did the same, our collective hearts pounding. "We're allowed to be here, yet we're skulking around like we're breaking and entering."

"Rich people are weird," Poppy said. "They like to keep their stuff private at all costs. Even if their daughter said we could come here, they could claim she's lying if they wanted to."

"Do you think we should leave?" Yasmine asked. "This feels a little bizarre. I've never done anything like this before."

Annabel shook her head. "I agree with my sister. Rich people are weird, but no one seems to be here. I think we're safe, at least until morning."

"Not only am I giving Marco our location," I told everyone, "I'm sending it through Find My Phone so he can see us moment to moment. And I agree with Yasmine that this is a little bizarre. We're sneaking around this massive yard in the dark with no clue what we're doing."

"This location is horror-movie ideal," Poppy said. "If we all screamed, I'm not sure anybody would hear us."

"You Google Earthed this," I said after I'd sent Marco my location, okaying it for the next twenty-four hours. "There are literally tons of people living all around here."

"I'm not seeing any lockbox Kelly described," Yasmine said. "I think this is the service entrance." She gestured toward another door that was tucked away.

I went close to the house to peer through the window next to the door. Without putting my hand on the glass, I leaned in as close as I could. "I think this is the kitchen, or at least a staff kitchen, so that makes sense. When they entertain, the catering staff probably comes through here."

"I wonder where the catering staff would come into one of those efficiency apartments." Annabel chortled. "Just kidding. There's only one entrance."

"Let's walk around to the other side," Poppy suggested. "Then we can see if there are any other doors with lockboxes."

Annabel followed, punching two fists in the air. "I'm ready to fend off the gerbils."

CHAPTER 8

We found refuge on some beautiful outdoor couches nestled in a secluded corner by a crazy-enormous pool. This area had a massive outdoor stone fireplace with a giant TV hung over it.

We had not discovered a way into the home.

Kelly had responded to one of Yasmine's texts, reiterating that the lockbox was at the service entrance. Yasmine had gone to recheck.

Poppy was sprawled on one couch, her elbow draped over her eyes. "So close, yet so far."

"If Yasmine doesn't find the lockbox," I said, "we can just sleep out here. It's plenty warm enough, and there's tons of room on all these couches."

"Sorry, sis," Annabel said. "You might not get to caress those cabinets after all."

Something unintelligible came out of Poppy's mouth, followed by a moan.

Yasmine came back a few minutes later, shaking her head. "I don't see any of what Kelly's describing. She said the door is black, and it's near the southeast corner of the house."

"Maybe we are indeed at the wrong house?" Annabel suggested.

"Impossible." Poppy struggled up on her elbows. "I put the address Kelly sent to Yasmine in my maps app after we got coffee this morning." That felt like a hundred million years ago. It'd been a very long day. "This is the house that came up. Plus, Marley, Yasmine's friend, told her that this house was literally right next door to Meghan and Harry." She collapsed back down. "Google Earth says we're in the right place."

"Google Earth is not infallible," Annabel reminded her. "But I agree with Eve. We can sleep out here on these couches. They're hella comfortable and probably cost three times what a regular indoor couch costs. Then we can figure it out in the morning and hightail it out of here if we're in the wrong place."

"What do you want to do?" I asked Yasmine.

This was her mission after all.

She sat on one of the massive cushions. There were two U-shaped couches back-to-back. It was a huge, cozy space. "I'm so close to achieving my goal. If I give up now, and we can't get back here, I could definitely miss my opportunity. But I don't want to get any of us in trouble if we're in the wrong place."

"What if we try to pass the bodyguards the letter and the knife tonight?" I suggested. "If we do that, we have a chance to sneak out before anyone is the wiser."

"You want to do it now?" Yasmine asked, raising her eyebrows.

"Sure, why not?" I replied. "Maybe the night-shift bodyguard rotation is a little more laid-back? They might only have one or two people on duty. We don't even know if Meghan or Harry are in town. After we deliver the stuff, we can decide if we want to leave, and then you won't miss your opportunity."

Annabel stood. "I like it. Adrenaline is still pumping through my veins." She shook her arms out. "If anything, we can do reconnaissance and get the lay of the land and be ready for an early-morning mission."

"It's pitch-black out here." Poppy flung an arm over her head to point at the bushes. "We're going to be bumbling around out there with only our phones to guide us."

"Honestly," I told her, "that's better than us being in the wrong place, and staff coming tomorrow to witness us creeping across the yard like characters in a Scooby-Doo cartoon. No one is on the premises right now. No lights are on in the house. There doesn't seem to be a caretaker, or I'm pretty sure they would've noticed us already. I say we take our opportunity and run with it."

Yasmine stood. "I'm all for that. I'm also sending Kelly our location so she can verify. I should've done that earlier. But she hasn't been very responsive."

Poppy rolled off the couch. "Okay. Let's do this thing. I'm taking a selfie at the property line, just so everyone knows. With a flash."

"I think we're pretty close to the border," Annabel said, checking her phone. She motioned at the trees and hedges to the right of where we were sitting. "I say we go straight through there and take a look around."

We left all of our things on the couches and followed Annabel across the short expanse. There was no way to penetrate the wall of hedges once we arrived. We saw no nooks or crannies to slide through. It was too dense.

"Let's head this way." Yasmine motioned. "I think I saw a gap up by the parking area near the house."

We continued walking.

"Where's Poppy?" I asked, suddenly realizing she wasn't with us.

We all stopped.

"I'm in here," a muffled voice called. "I found a hole." Snapping and crackling followed. "Dang, it's thick in here."

Gathering in front of the very small opening Poppy had managed to wiggle her body into, we crouched down.

"I can't fit through there," Annabel said. "It's only big enough for hobbits."

"Oh crap," Poppy cried. "I hit something." It sounded like she was patting her hand against hard surface. "It's a stone wall. No way I'm getting over that. But I can keep crawling forward. There's kind of a tunnel."

"Maybe you should come out," I told her. "There's no way we can come in after you. You're the smallest among us, so if you—"

"I see a way through," she exclaimed excitedly.

More snapping and crackling sounded.

Then one of the hedges began to shake.

"Are you climbing the branches?" Annabel asked. "Be careful. They're not meant to hold human weight. Even though you're hobbit-sized, you could—"

A crash followed, then a loud *ooof.*

"Poppy!" I cried, much louder than a whisper-yell. "Are you okay? Where did you land?" I tried to peer through the wall of darkness. "We can't see you from here."

The three of us shone our phone lights into the thicket, but there were too many deep shadows.

"Are you hurt?" Yasmine called. "Please tell us!"

"What's going on?" Annabel asked. "You better say something soon, or we're calling 911."

"I'm…okay," Poppy replied, her voice farther away than before. "I just got the breath knocked out of me. Give me a second." More rustling. "I think…I think I'm on the other side. I did it! Oh my *God*. I'm here. I'm really—"

"Trespassing," Annabel finished, moving to the left slightly to try to hear her sister better. "I'm not sure that was the plan."

"What do you mean?" Poppy called in a slightly panicked voice. "We were trying to get through the hedges. I did it. I got through!"

I bit my lip. "I think what Annabel means is that we were going to, like, go up to the line and maybe try to flag someone down, but not exactly cross over onto their property." I glanced at Yasmine and Annabel standing next to me, then I shrugged. "To be fair, we hadn't sussed it all out yet. I'm sure it's going to be fine."

"Well, I can't get back the way I came. I basically fell through a tree, and there's no way to climb back."

"Are you in more hedges?" Annabel called. "Or are you standing in their yard? Tell us, what can you see?"

"I'm in between two trees," Poppy said. "They're not exactly hedges. They're more spaced apart, but still sort of hedge-like."

"Can you duck behind them and keep out of sight?" Annabel asked.

"I think so," Poppy replied. "I'm a little scared to use my

phone light. I really don't want to be arrested. Am I going to get arrested?"

Her panic was intensifying at a quick rate.

"You're not getting arrested," I soothed. "We're all going to walk toward the parking area. You follow on that side. There's bound to be a place where you can climb back over."

"There's an opening near the corner of the property," Yasmine told Poppy. "I saw it the second time I went to look at the service door."

"Okay," Poppy replied. "There's enough ambient light for me to see in between these trees. It's not as dark as the hedgerow."

We all began walking.

Less than a minute into our journey, Poppy gave a soft shriek.

"*What?*" Both Annabel and I whisper-shouted at the same time, stopping and shining our lights into the hedges to no avail.

"I can see the play yard," Poppy said excitedly. "Where little Archie and Lili probably play. I don't think I'm near the house, though." We heard relief coupled with disappointment in her voice.

Annabel leaned toward my ear. "If she gets arrested for trespassing, how much jail time are we talking?"

I gaped at her. "She's not getting jail time! That would be…"

"Trespassing is a misdemeanor in California," Yasmine whispered. "This is not what I wanted to happen. I literally just thought we'd lean over the fence and hand somebody a letter." She sucked in a breath. "And a freaking knife! What was I thinking?" She covered her face with her hands. "It sounded so much better in my mind. This is all my fault. She's going to go to jail, and it's all going to be my fault."

"This is not on you," I told Yasmine, my voice brooking no

room for argument. "It was an excellent plan. It still is. We can execute it. We're all here by choice. In fact, Poppy basically forced her way onto this trip. She's a big girl. She made her own choices, beginning with tunneling through the hedges and falling out on the other side like Velma trying to solve a cartoon mystery. But, even better, we're going to get her out of there before anybody notices, and then we'll regroup. We will fix this. We *will* get your letter to Matt. Maybe you keep the pocketknife and give it to him after he reads the letter. Just to be on the safe side."

"Yeah, that sounds good." Yasmine nodded.

"Where are you guys?" Poppy's voice was farther away, somewhere ahead of us.

We hurried to catch up.

"We're right here," Annabel called, using her phone flashlight to illuminate the area in front of her. "Can you see the light?"

"Faintly," Poppy replied.

"I can see the parking pad up ahead," Annabel told her. "We're almost there. Do not go full Muppet on us. Do you hear me? We need you in a fully functioning body to get you out of there."

"I'm not going to—" A small shriek sounded.

"What? What happened?" I cried.

"Did someone see you?" Yasmine called.

"I tripped," Poppy said. "There are so many roots—"

She stopped speaking abruptly.

"What now?" Annabel asked. "What are you—"

"*Shhhh.* I hear voices," Poppy hissed.

I strained, but I couldn't hear anything. "Are you sure?"

"Yes," Poppy said, her voice a little closer. A loud crack came from nearby. "I'm trying to get back through, but the hedges on your side are too thick."

"Don't waste your time trying to fight the trees," Annabel told her. "Just hightail it down to the end."

"But—"

"Don't argue," Annabel insisted. "Just do it."

"Okay."

My phone pinged with a text from Marco. The screen was facing me because I had my light shining on the ground.

ARE YOU IN A YARD OR SOMETHING? I'VE BEEN WATCHING YOUR LOCATION NOW FOR THE LAST TEN MINUTES. I PULLED UP GOOGLE MAPS, BUT I CAN'T FIGURE OUT WHERE YOU ARE.

I'm certain it looked strange that we were very slowly walking between two large houses at almost one in the morning.

I texted him back as we walked.

WE'RE WALKING. POPPY'S CURRENTLY LOST IN THE BUSHES.

He responded quickly.

LOST IN THE BUSHES?

HARD TO EXPLAIN. WE WEREN'T ACTUALLY TRYING TO GET INTO THE NEXT YARD, JUST GET SOMEBODY'S ATTENTION. BUT POPPY FOUND HER WAY THROUGH, AND SHE CAN'T GET BACK.

I stopped abruptly so I wouldn't crash into Annabel.

We'd reached the area Yasmine had mentioned.

A second later, Poppy's face came into view.

"Oh, thank goodness," she cried. She had a few twigs in her hair and appeared a little disheveled. "I was thinking I'd never find a way out."

"I'm so glad you're okay," Yasmine said, rushing toward her.

Right as Poppy lifted her leg to make it over the stone wall that we could now see, a super-authoritative voice shouted from behind her, "Stop right there!"

CHAPTER 9

W e all froze and put our hands in the air.

Even though bodyguards were not the same as police officers, it just felt like the right thing to do.

A second later, the beam from a large flashlight was aimed right at the three of us on one side, Poppy still on the other, her back to us now.

Several men were jogging over, the one in the lead calling, "Stay right where you are!"

They were at least fifty yards away.

Annabel leaned in. "Welp, I guess we found the bodyguards."

They looked exactly how you'd expect bodyguards to look. Each of them wore dark clothing, likely suits, but I couldn't see from this distance, and they were all large. One of them was a little shorter than the other two.

Marco's text sound chimed.

I HOPE YOU GET WHERE YOU NEED TO GO.

Without thinking, I texted back as quickly as I could: PROBABLY GOING TO JAIL.

Annabel moved closer to the wall.

I whispered, "What are you doing?"

"If my sister's going to jail, so am I. Right now, she's the only one trespassing. But not for long." Annabel settled her butt on the top of the wall and pivoted quickly, shifting cleanly to the other side.

The bodyguards were closing in.

Yasmine and I looked at each other.

I shrugged, perched on top of the wall, and lifted my legs. "You stay on this side," I told her. "We'll try to reason with them."

She shook her head vigorously. "No way. All for one and one for all." She hopped over, landing next to me.

The first of the bodyguards got to us. He wasn't even out of breath. "You guys are trespassing on private property," he told us sternly. He was the one holding the flashlight. It was now aimed at our feet.

Two more security guards caught up. One was speaking on a walkie-talkie.

I guess they still used those.

Hoping to explain before things escalated, I said, "We aren't here to bother Meghan and—"

"You're going to have to come with us," the short one interrupted in a semigrowl, his hands on his hips as he scrutinized us.

"Let us explain," Annabel said. "Honestly, we're just here to get a note to—"

"The cops are already on their way," the middle one said after dropping his walkie-talkie.

"There's been a mistake," Poppy started. "This is all my fault. See, we're staying with Kelly and her family"—she gestured at the house behind us—"and I got a little too excited when I found out the duke and duchess live next door. So we were just trying to get a glimpse, and I accidentally fell through the hedges. My friends were just trying to help me back over."

That sounded totally sane. *Yay, Poppy.*

The guy with the flashlight folded his arms. He was the oldest and seemed like he was in charge. He was also very annoyed.

It's too bad they didn't have name tags. That would've made things easier.

"You're trespassing on private property," the folded-arms guy said. "It doesn't matter what your intentions were."

"Please," Yasmine said. "This is all *my* fault. We came here because I'm trying to find Matt Gallagher. We don't want anything to do with the duke and duchess. I just really wanted to give him a message. Is he here?"

The eyebrows of the guy with the walkie-talkie shot up when he heard Matt's name.

"Enough talking," the short guy said. "You need to come with us."

"Isn't there some sort of due process?" Annabel questioned. "We're literally one foot over the property line, and we're guests of the residents who live in that house." She pointed behind us. "There is no need to take us to jail."

The first guy squinted at us, dropping his arms. "You're guests of the Crawfords?" There was an unmistakable challenge in his voice.

We all glanced at Yasmine, as we didn't know Kelly's last name.

"Yes," Yasmine said. "Their daughter Kelly gave us permission to be here."

The guy looked at the man with the walkie-talkie. "Do they have a daughter named Kelly?"

The guy shrugged. "I have no idea. But it doesn't matter. We're hired to do a job. They're on our property, and they don't have permission to be here." He began to walk, gesturing. "Come with us quietly, and there won't be any problems."

We all looked at one another, but we had no choice but to follow. It's not like we were going to somehow outrun these guys.

My phone had gone off a number of times as Marco tried to get a hold of me, including calling once. I was so distraught that I'd only scanned the messages, but didn't reply. He was inquiring about our safety and wondering what was going on.

He'd be able to see my phone location as we moved farther onto the other property, and that made me feel better. He'd just have to wait until I had a moment to text him back.

It took us a while to get off the lawn, then we walked past a row of garages and into a small room. Two other security guards were inside.

"Tony, go down to the gate and escort the police up," the lead guy with the flashlight told one of the men inside the room. Tony left immediately.

"Have a seat," the shorter guy said, gesturing idly at a few folding chairs against one wall.

The room was no bigger than my bedroom at home, so it was quite cramped with all of us inside. One long desk ran under two small windows.

"Listen," Poppy started as we sat, "we didn't mean to trespass. Like my friend here told you, we're just trying to get a note to Matt Gallagher. Can you tell us if he's working tonight? That would help a lot."

"How do you know Matt?" the guy with the walkie-talkie asked.

Hope welled in my chest that maybe we could wiggle out of this. I glanced at Yasmine. This was her story.

She cleared her throat. "Matt and I…used to be involved. I don't have his contact information and just found out a week ago that he's working for the duke and duchess. A friend of mine put me in touch with Kelly Crawford, and we decided to drive down this weekend." She slid a folded envelope out of her back pocket. They hadn't searched us, so I assumed they didn't think we were an actual threat. "I was hoping to give him this. And that's literally it."

The guy was starting to look sympathetic, but not overly so. "This is not the way to go about getting someone a message."

"Why not?" Annabel challenged. "Matt's not on social media, and no one has his number. As invited guests of the people next door, it seemed like a good idea to us."

"We're not in the business of passing notes." The shorter one scowled. He was extremely irritated that we'd ruined his night. That much was clear.

"The police have been summoned," the guy with the walkie-talkie said. "Even if we had a change of heart, we can't let you go. Once you crossed onto this property, you broke the law. It's our job to make sure that doesn't happen. If we don't follow through, we wouldn't be doing our jobs."

"But we didn't mean to," Poppy insisted. "That has to count for something. I'm the only one who was on the wrong side to begin with. And that was a mistake. I was crawling through the hedges, and a branch broke. It dumped me on this property. I was just trying to get back. My friends jumped over at the last minute so I wouldn't have to go through this alone. We were over the line by, like, a foot."

The lead guy's eyebrows rose. "You were crawling through the hedges? That sounds like intent to trespass to me."

"The only intent we had," I countered, "was to get that note to Matt. I'm sure you get a lot of crazies around here trying to sneak in to get a glimpse of the duke and duchess, but that's not us. We meant no harm to them. We were just trying to help out a friend."

The walkie-talkie in his hand cracked, and a voice came out. "Cops are here. Bring them down."

We all shuffled out, uncertain of what was to come.

They hadn't asked for our names or searched us. This was so surreal. I'd never been arrested before.

As we walked, Annabel asked, "So now what? Do we get charged? When do they let us out? Are we going to have to spend the night in jail?"

"The police will take you down to the local station and process you," the lead guy said. "Then it depends on what the owners want to do."

Owners meaning Meghan and Harry.

"They're not currently in the country," he went on, "so it's going to take a few hours minimum to work it all out. We'll probably get a hold of the Crawfords and see if your story checks out." He gave us a look that said he highly doubted it would check out. "If it does, you'll likely get out with a slap on the wrist. That's your best-case scenario. In the future, do not try to deliver messages by trespassing."

"Understood, sir," Yasmine said. "I take full responsibility for this plan. It was a mistake to think it would work, and you have my sincere apologies. I only wanted to get an important message to Matt. It won't happen again."

There were two cop cars parked near the gates. Four cops total.

With little fanfare and not much interaction, they ushered Yasmine and Annabel into the back of one cruiser and Poppy and me into the other.

"This is all my fault," Poppy whisper-moaned. "If I hadn't screwed up, we wouldn't be in this position. I got too caught up in the moment. I wish I could take it all back."

"None of this feels real," I told her. "As soon as we pulled up in front of that gate, it's like we stepped into the Twilight Zone. Seeing how all of the bodyguards reacted to our plan, I realized it was silly of us to think it would've worked in the first place. But it's not only your fault. We were all running around like we were in a spy movie. These bodyguards were not having it."

"Yeah, they take their jobs pretty seriously," Poppy said miserably. "Do you think we're going to get convicted?"

I shook my head. "I can't imagine we will, but I have no idea."

The ride to the station was very short. We pulled up in front of a two-story white stucco building. Very California. The cops barely said anything to us as they shuffled us into the station. They made us remove any personal items, including our phones, and put them in envelopes. We didn't have our purses on us, as they were back at the home on the couches next to the pool. The cops told us someone was going to go collect them.

Before I handed over my phone, I very quickly texted Marco without reading through what he'd written to me, which was quite a lot.

will call u when i can. at the jail. am ok.

A female police officer led us down a hallway into a back room where there were two cells. She opened the larger cell and directed us all inside. Three benches lined the walls, and there was a sink in the corner. That was it.

"Sit tight," she told us. "Not sure if we're going to process you tonight or not."

"Does everybody who trespasses get charged?" Annabel asked. "I'm assuming you see quite a few people like us."

She appeared wistful for a second. "You're certainly not our first. But up until a few years ago, this wasn't a thing."

I understood the implication. Having the royals in town had shaken things up.

"Justin, the lead security guard, is following up on a few things. Once he gets back to us, we'll know how to proceed. It's our understanding that you were barely over the property line and were guests of the neighbors. We'll see how it plays out. But I'd suggest you try and get as comfortable as you can. It's the middle of the night, and getting a hold of people who are out of the country takes time."

We all took a seat.

Yasmine set her head in her hands. "I can't believe I thought this was a good idea. I'm so sorry, you guys." She glanced up, misty-eyed. "If my parents find out about this, it's going to be ten times worse than when I tell them I'm no longer engaged. They're going to be so disappointed. They'll probably insist I move to Morocco so they can keep a better eye on me. I've never broken the law in my life, much less gone to jail."

Poppy shifted over on the bench, wrapping her arm around Yasmine, shaking her shoulder in a total Poppy way. "They're not going to find out. It's okay," she soothed. "If I have to, I'll literally fall to my knees in front of the magistrate and confess that I was the only one who was trespassing. Because that's the truth. And I always speak the truth."

"I can attest to that," Annabel said. "She's very truthy."

Poppy continued, "I made the very stupid choice to crawl into the bushes all on my own. None of you asked for any of this. My only excuse is that I was blinded by my need to see all things Meghan and Harry. If we'd stayed on our side and shouted at one of those guys to come over, everything would be completely fine. This is not anyone's fault but mine."

Annabel snorted. "Those guys were never going to help us. They thought our little scheme was ridiculous."

"I don't know," I mused. "The one with the walkie-talkie seemed a little sympathetic toward the end. I have a feeling he's a friend of Matt's. When you mentioned Matt, his expression changed. He totally knows him."

"They were just following protocol," Yasmine said. "Which means they probably wouldn't have interacted with us at all, even if we'd called them, if given the choice. I'm so dumb, because I know that from dating a bodyguard. The plan was flawed from the start. Then, to make matters worse, we left all of our stuff in the portico by the pool. Your car is still at the gate." She nodded to Poppy. "This is an unmitigated disaster. I'm taking the blame. If my parents taught me anything, it was to own up to my shortcomings, and this was an epic fail on my part."

"You didn't fail," I assured her.

Annabel started to giggle.

We all stared.

Then she began to laugh harder, slapping her thigh.

"What in the world is so funny?" Poppy asked, sounding irritated.

"I'm not laughing at anything in particular. I swear," Annabel hooted. "It's just…this is going to be the funniest story to retell we've ever had. Does anything top being thrown in jail for trying to sneak into a royal's front yard?" More laughter. "We'll be telling it for years. The part about you falling out of the hedges is the best part." She was clutching her stomach, rocking back and forth. "You…you literally squeezed through an opening the size of a dog door and then thought to yourself, 'Why not climb up this rickety hedge? I'm sure the thin branches will hold me.' Then you crash-landed on your face—"

Poppy sputtered as we all joined in the laughter. "I don't need to have it described to me. I lived it." Then she began to laugh, rocking Yasmine along with her. "Oh my goodness, what was I *thinking*? If anyone has to own up to their shortcomings, it's me!"

"That's because"—Annabel drummed her feet on the ground—"you're short!"

We laughed ourselves silly for about ten minutes, each of us hooting about a particular point in the story. What else did you do in jail except try to laugh at yourself?

The adrenaline had to exit our bodies somehow.

I wiped tears from my eyes. "It's two thirty in the morning, and we just drove sixteen hours straight, with only a single burger to fuel us. We should try to get some sleep."

Poppy looked aghast. "Sleep? Here? Surely you jest. There's no way any of us are getting any sleep."

"I don't know about that," Annabel said as she stretched out on the bench, using her arm as a pillow. "I can pretty much sleep anywhere."

I yawned. "This is not quite the night I'd envisioned, but if I have to spend time in jail, I'm glad it's with you ladies." I eased back, crossing my arms across my chest, my back resting against the wall.

"Perp besties for life," Poppy said as she yawned herself. "Pretty soon, we won't even know what life looks like on the outside."

"I call laundry duty," Annabel said tiredly, readjusting herself as she closed her eyes. "I hope they stick me with a cellmate that looks just like Molly Ringwald."

CHAPTER 10

The jangling of keys woke me up, which was stereotypical for prison, but one hundred percent accurate. Footsteps were coming our way. I sat up slowly, feeling groggy and out of it. My eyes burned. Sleep had been fitful, but I'd definitely gotten some z's in there, which seemed like a miracle, considering

I was certain if we hadn't just driven sixteen hours, sleep would've been impossible.

"What time is it?" Poppy asked in a tired voice.

"Not sure," I answered quietly.

Annabel and Yasmine were still asleep, both sprawled at either end of the same bench, their feet almost touching.

"I can't believe I was actually able to get any rest, but I did," Poppy murmured. "But man, my back feels like somebody drop-kicked it, then stomped on it a few times."

"Mine, too," I said, reaching around to rub it. I could honestly say that I'd never slept sitting up in a jail cell before.

It was something I hoped never to revisit.

"Yasmine?" a male voice called. A tall, dark-haired man entered the room slightly ahead of the female officer who accompanied him. He was at least six five with broad shoulders and a very chiseled chin. His hair was cut short, but styled a little longer on top. He was stunningly handsome. He could be the next Jack Reacher. Maybe he was? We were close to Hollywood after all. "Yasmine, is that you?"

"Matt?" Yasmine struggled to sit up, obviously trying to figure out where she was. "Is it really you?"

He came close to the bars, grabbing hold of them as Yasmine rushed forward. "I came as soon as they told me you were here," he replied. "They took their sweet time telling me what happened, and I'm a little pissed. Gavin just got off his shift and decided to drop by instead of calling me. He told me the whole story while I was getting ready for work. I came straight over."

"I'm so sorry," she started. "This whole thing blew up. I was just trying to get a letter to you. It was so stupid." She shook her head. "I should've known better."

Poppy joined me on my bench, leaning over to whisper, "This is totally playing like a scene out of a movie. The ex-cop comes to rescue his wrongly accused woman. Except he's not a police officer, and she was rightly accused. And can I just say, she did not prepare us for how ridiculously good-looking he is. Holy cats. *Meeeow.*"

"He's pretty dreamy," I whispered back. "And he looks excited to see her."

"Totally," Poppy said. "I know a love face when I see one, and his is on point."

"A love face? You just made that up."

"Did not. Just look. He's moony-eyed, at the same time hungry, at the same time protective. Like, he can't wait to gobble her up, and if anybody gets in his way, he's ready to do some harm with those big guns of his. *Pow, pow.*" She mocked taking a few punches.

I sized him up.

He and Yasmine were murmuring to each other in low tones. He was intently focused on her, like nothing else existed. I was pretty sure he didn't know the rest of us were in here.

The cop next to him seemed to catch on to what was happening and graciously gave them their space.

Annabel waggled her eyebrows at us from across the cell, then flashed a double thumbs-up.

After a moment, Yasmine took a step back.

Matt addressed the rest of us. "You're all getting out of here. No charges will be filed."

We all perked up.

"They got a hold of the duke and duchess?" Poppy asked, hope leaking around her worried tone. It would be another good story.

"I'm not sure of the particulars," Matt replied, glancing at the police officer. "But I think the Crawfords vouched for you. That was enough."

"Kelly came through in the end," Annabel said as she stood, stretching her arms over her head. "That means we were at the right house. I didn't expect that plot twist, but it's a good one. Kept us out of the clink long term."

The police officer unlocked the cell. "Follow me," she said. "We'll get all your personal items back to you, and you're free to go."

"What time is it?" I asked as we shuffled out.

"It's about six forty-five," Matt replied. "Oh, and by the way, there's another dude sitting in the holding area, waiting for you guys."

"Another dude?" I asked.

"For us?" Poppy asked. "Are you sure?"

"Maybe he brought burgers?" Annabel said. "Or perhaps a couple dozen Egg McMuffins? I'm so hungry. I'm pretty sure we ate at that diner forty-seven years ago."

"No food. But I believe he's here for you guys," Matt said. "He arrived an hour or so ago and asked about you, but they wouldn't give him any information. From what I've been told, he's just been patiently waiting."

My heart began to beat.

Yasmine and I exchanged glances. "It's probably Marco." She inclined her head in my direction. "You texted him our location, right?"

"I did." It wouldn't be hard for Marco to figure out where we were. It would be right there on his phone.

"Who's Marco?" Matt asked.

Yasmine and Matt had a lot to discuss, and none of us was going to spoil anything for her. A significant amount of time had passed since Yasmine and Matt had been together.

"Oh, he's my boyfriend," I replied nonchalantly.

It felt exhilarating to say that out loud, even if wasn't all the way true.

"And also my fiancé," Yasmine said.

"Your fiancé?" Matt's brows furrowed.

"Pretty much an ex-fiancé, but for breaking the news to their families," Annabel offered. "And it's not nearly as complicated as it sounds." This information was likely all in Yasmine's letter, but Matt didn't even have that in hand yet. "Yasmine and Marco were set up by their families, but they didn't make a love match. Instead, Marco fell for Eve"—she gestured at me—"and Yasmine realized that she was still in love with you"—she gestured at Matt—"so here we are."

Matt seemed stunned by the frank explanation.

Yasmine appeared pale.

"You guys have so much to catch up on!" Poppy cried, her voice nice and light while she ushered us forward with her arms spread wide, as we'd all kind of stalled in the hallway. "We're so excited that you two are going to get a chance to talk after all this time. But let's get our stuff first and, you know, settle up with the police, or whatever we're supposed to do here."

We followed the officer into a large room with a desk. She handed us the envelopes with our things in them. I hurried to get my phone out and was relieved to see it still had a charge.

There were several texts and missed calls from Marco, the last text being:

I'M ON MY WAY.

I couldn't believe he was actually here.

That meant he'd taken an early morning flight from Seattle to LA or Santa Barbara.

They officially released us, and we filed out into the main room.

Marco stood from where he'd been waiting in a chair near the door. I wasn't quite sure what to do or how to react. I felt like running and jumping into his arms, but I resisted. He looked tired, but totally adorable. He was dressed in a black button-up and dark jeans. It had to be completely weird for him to see his fiancée, her ex-boyfriend, and me all together.

Before either of us could decide how to proceed, a woman with long, wavy, blonde hair stood. She looked like California had literally given birth to her.

"Yasmine?" she asked, coming forward.

"Kelly?" Yasmine replied.

"Yes. It's me." She hurried over and gave Yasmine a quick hug. "I'm so, so sorry! This is all my fault. I should've given you better instructions. It turned out to be such a mess."

"It's not your fault," Yasmine assured her.

"I was totally distracted at work," Kelly continued. "Then my phone died. When I found out what happened, I tried to get a hold of my parents right away, but they didn't answer for a few hours. I've been back at the house, trying to sort it all out."

"I appreciate that. I'm happy your parents vouched for us," Yasmine said. "You did such a nice thing for me by offering their home in the first place, and we've never even met."

She grinned. It was surprising she didn't have a surfboard casually linked under one arm. "Marley is, like, my best friend in the whole world, and she adores you. She's been meaning to introduce us for years. I was so happy to help you." She glanced slyly at Matt, who was a few steps away, watching everything intently. "It looks like you accomplished your goal, so that's awesome."

"Um," Yasmine replied shyly. "It seems I did."

"How about we head outside?" Poppy said. "I think we could all use a little fresh air."

Kelly led the way. "You guys should totally come back to the house. I'm sure you're tired and hungry."

Annabel reached out to make sure her sister didn't stumble

as Poppy whipped her head around and mouthed, "We're going to the house!"

Once outside, I pulled Marco to the side.

I wanted to keep touching him—I wanted to know this was real—but I dropped my hand when we were a few feet away. "I can't believe you flew down here," I whispered. "That was so nice of you."

"Of course," he replied, as though jumping on a flight practically in the middle of the night was what people did every day. "When the last text I got from you said you were at the jail, I assumed that meant you'd been arrested, so I figured somebody would have to post bond or do something." He shrugged, shoving his hands in his pockets. It was a pose I'd gotten to know a lot over the last month and was one of my favorites. He was so endearing. "I wanted to make sure you and Yasmine were okay."

I glanced over at Yasmine, who was talking to Kelly. Poppy had her hands clasped in front of her chest, hanging on their every word.

"I'm so thankful you came," I told him. "I'm sure Yasmine is, too."

Was there a set precedent for proper interaction for something like this? Some sort of guidebook? Instructions on how to talk to your possibly new boyfriend while standing next to his soon-to-be ex-fiancée and her newly reconnected ex-boyfriend?

If there was one, I'd never heard about it.

Yasmine directed her attention to us. "Marco," she called. "I'd like you to meet Matt." She gestured at the large bodyguard standing to her left. "Matt, this is Marco Cruz, my *officially* soon-to-be ex-fiancé."

The two men graciously shook hands.

This was all very civilized and super-duper strange.

"We haven't told our families we've called it off," Marco clarified. "But we split amicably a little while ago."

"Because he and Eve were caught necking in the closet," Poppy added gleefully.

"Poppy!" I cried.

"I'm sorry," she said quickly, settling her fingers over her lips sheepishly. "It just slipped out." She glanced at Matt and then Kelly. "I'm not someone who usually airs dirty laundry, especially if it's not my own, in front of strangers. I apologize. Marco and Eve actually met eight years ago and sort of fell in love then. Well, at least Eve did. They've been reconnecting over the past few weeks after they went into business together— they're opening this super-cute floral shop called the Watering Can—which has caused them to spend *a lot* of time together. So, you know, it became clear that Yasmine and Marco would split, which, in turn, left Yasmine open to come here and find her true—"

My eyes slid shut. This wasn't happening.

"Okay!" Annabel interjected, moving quickly toward her sister. "I think we've done enough damage for one day, or possibly the entire week, or maybe the year. It's more than time to bail on this jail."

Matt rubbed the back of his neck. "Yeah, I say we get out of here."

I'm sure it'd been a lot for him to hear.

"Do you have to go back to work?" Yasmine asked Matt.

"Not right this minute," he replied. "Gavin is covering my

morning shift, and I'll relieve him around lunchtime. It was the least he could do after waiting so long to tell me what was up."

"I bet you guys are starving," Kelly said. "Let's head to the house, and you can fill me in on what happened. It sounds kind of exciting!"

"We should stop and pick up some food first," Annabel said. "We don't want to put you out. I could eat like three horses."

Kelly swished her hand. "It's not a problem. Our cook came in today. She's preparing a big breakfast. I told her to expect at least four. But I'm sure she'll have enough on hand for everyone."

I raised my eyebrows. "Um, that's so kind of you, but—"

"You really don't have to host us," Yasmine cut in, obviously thinking the same thing I was.

Having somebody else's chef cook for us felt a little weird, like it'd be intrusive.

"I insist," Kelly said. "Plus, you have to come back to the house anyway to get your things and your car. You can also sneak more of a peek at the yard of the duke and duchess, without getting arrested this time." She waggled her eyebrows. "I know where the gaps in the hedges are. The views are pretty incredible. I still can't believe my parents bought the house next door."

House was such an inadequate word for that megamansion.

I glanced at Poppy, who was literally throbbing with anticipation, but doing a good job of keeping her mouth shut this time. She was waiting for Yasmine to decide, since all of this was for her and Matt.

"Okay, yeah, that sounds okay," Yasmine said.

"My car is just down the street," Kelly said.

"So is mine," Matt said.

Marco cleared his throat. "My rental is also parked on the street."

Annabel clapped her hands. "Okay, Poppy and I will go with Kelly. Yasmine and Matt can ride together. Eve and Marco can follow. Sound good, everyone?"

Bless her for taking the reins.

"Yes, that sounds perfect," I said. "We'll see you there."

Chapter 11

In Marco's rental car, a black four-door sedan much like his own at home, I buckled up. I wasn't sure what to say. I settled on, "This is so weird."

Marco blew out a short breath, cracking a smile. 'It's literally the weirdest situation I've ever been in my entire life." He started the car by pressing a button. "But I'm so glad you're okay and nothing terrible happened."

"Me, too," I said. "Have you ever jumped on a plane that quickly before?"

"Never," he said, pulling out to follow Kelly, who drove a bright yellow sports car of some kind that was no doubt very expensive. "It all worked out seamlessly, which was surprising. The flight was leaving in an hour and had a few seats on it. I just sort of ran out the door."

"It was so unbelievably sweet of you to come running," I said, feeling lame that the conversation sounded so banal. We'd known each other for what seemed like an eon, but we didn't really *know* each other, and we weren't in a relationship. Yet.

"Were you scared?" he asked.

"Not terribly," I told him.

He made a few turns, following Kelly, and I suddenly realized I didn't want this important, new kind of interaction with Marco to happen in front of everyone, especially not Yasmine and Matt, who had their own awkward terrain to navigate. "You know what? How about we head to the beach or somewhere else instead?"

"Really?" He glanced at me quickly, seeming completely relieved.

"Yeah. We need to have a real conversation, and we won't be able to do it at Kelly's. I'm ready to be done with this whole ordeal, if I'm being honest. We accomplished what we set out to do—Yasmine and Matt have reconnected. Not to mention, I don't need to see the inside of that house." I pulled my phone out and texted Poppy to let her know Marco and I were going to deviate from the plan.

Marco took a right, angling us toward the coast.

Poppy texted back.

I TOTALLY UNDERSTAND! WILL GRAB ALL YOUR STUFF.

I thanked her.

She followed up with:

ARE YOU DRIVING BACK TO SEATTLE WITH MARCO? OR FLYING? OR DO YOU GUYS WANT TO RIDE WITH US?

I looked over at Marco. "Poppy wants to know if we want to ride back with them. Did you book a round-trip ticket?"

He shook his head. "I booked a one-way ticket. The rental car company said I could drop this off at the Seattle airport if I wanted to, for an extra charge. I wasn't sure if you"—he cleared his throat—"would want to drive back with me or not."

"Driving back with you sounds lovely. I'll tell Poppy."

My stomach fluttered as I texted her. Riding back with him would mean a possible overnight stay somewhere.

Poppy replied with hearts and smiley-face kissing emojis, then a row of eggplants, followed by a row of water drops.

Leave it to Poppy to cut right to the chase.

I burst out laughing.

"What?" Marco asked.

"Oh, it's just Poppy being completely inappropriate and hilarious, as always." I put my phone down. I didn't want Marco to see her texts right at this very moment.

"When I came in from the airport, I saw a restaurant with a view of the ocean that didn't look very busy. They had a big sign advertising breakfast. How does that sound?"

"Perfect. I'm starving."

We sat in comfortable silence as he drove. We had so much to say to each other, but we were content to just be for a moment.

All of our interactions over the past month had been electrically charged with desire tempered by caution. It was hard to believe we were finally free to explore our feelings without guilt or shame.

It was completely amazing.

"Here we are," Marco said as he pulled into a lot that was about a quarter full. It was still early in the morning. But since it was Sunday, I was certain other customers would be arriving soon.

We walked in, and the hostess seated us at a booth next to the window. The ocean was off in the distance and was completely beautiful. The early morning sun glinted off the white foam. Seagulls swooped for fish. A light breeze wafted through the palm leaves.

We both ordered eggs, toast, and hash browns. Marco got a large orange juice, and I got coffee. We made some small talk, catching up. We talked about the shop and the upcoming deliveries.

"I don't know if you remember this," he said, setting down his juice, "but on the first day we worked together at the bookstore, you spotted me a twenty."

"I do remember." I smiled. He'd been so adorable. I'd been enamored of him from the very beginning, the instant I'd seen him. It'd felt like the universe had opened up and dropped him into my life.

"It blew me away that you would do that. I'm pretty sure I made some dumb comment about not having enough money to buy a school sweatshirt, but now that I had a job at the bookstore, I could get it at a discount. At the end of our shift, you handed me the money. I tried to give it back to you, but you insisted I keep it. You said you wanted me to be able to wear the sweatshirt to the first football game, which every freshman went to dressed up in school spirit. In that moment, I fell for you."

You did? freshman me was screaming.

"Those feelings overwhelmed me. They scared the absolute crap out of me. I'd never gone on a date before, and here I was dreaming about being with you." He grinned. I was mesmerized. "You were completely out of my league. Beautiful, confident, generous, and obviously savvy. For you, it was no big deal to give me your money. For me, it was absolutely everything." He took a bite of his hash browns, seeming to contemplate what he would say next.

I dipped my toast in an egg yolk, eager to hear whatever it was.

"My parents did the best they could when I was young, but we never had any money to spare. Some months, they barely scraped by, always living paycheck to paycheck. Growing up poor has been a constant driving force in my life. The need to break that cycle and succeed has always been at the forefront of my mind. When your parents each speak in a different accent and constantly struggle to put basic necessities on the table, it sets you apart. My lack of socialization and that feeling of otherness always made me self-conscious. Your act of selflessness triggered me to break out of my box even more. You set me on the path I'm on today, and I'm grateful for it. After that day at the bookstore, I wanted to impress you. I wanted you to like me. Most of all, I wanted to prove to you that I could succeed. That I could be the one who could give you a twenty if you needed it."

He'd given me so much more. He'd invested in my dream to open a flower shop.

Tears gathered at the corners of my eyes. I'd had no idea that my gift back then had made such an impact. It was a little humbling to know that I'd affected somebody's life so profoundly. "If I recollect correctly," I said, "you repaid me at our next shift together. You were also wearing the sweatshirt. You looked cute in it."

"I sold my sound system to my roommate so I could pay you back immediately."

I gasped, pressing steepled fingers to my lips. "Oh no! Please tell me that's not true. That's not what I wanted at all. You could've paid me back at a much later date. I'm so sorry you felt pressure to repay me so quickly."

"It was my choice." He grabbed my hand across the table and brought it to his lips, kissing it. My entire body melted. "Like I said, I wanted to impress you. *Needed* to impress you. I wanted to validate your kindness by wearing the sweatshirt. In my sheltered mind, it was a way to tell you that I could support the woman I cared for. That I had means. And it worked. I missed my sound system, but I learned that I could easily live without it. Your act of kindness changed how I thought about my life at the very core. It shaped me for the better. Please don't apologize."

"I feel like I might've emasculated you, which was not my intent at all."

"No. You taught me not to covet unnecessary things, to work hard, to set a goal and meet it. But"—he chuckled—"I continued to be intimidated by you. You were, and still are, so confident and full of life. It's infectious. I knew you had feelings for me. Your flirting was the highlight of my life. I couldn't believe you were interested in me. But the young, unseasoned, video-game-coding junkie in me was terrified. The pressure was too intense. So instead of acting on the chemistry between us, I requested to work at a different bookstore on campus, claiming that I couldn't get to my classes on time. I didn't know what to do with my feelings back then." He flashed me a brilliant smile as he took a swig of his juice. "But I do now."

I was pretty sure the core of my being blushed. "That's good to know."

My phone beeped with a text from Poppy.

OMG! THIS PLACE IS INCREDIBLE. I DON'T WANT YOU TO MISS OUT.

A bunch of pictures followed.

I held up my phone so Marco could see.

The house was utterly gorgeous. Exactly how you'd think a megamansion would look. All the furniture was impeccable, the walls decorated in expensive-looking wallpaper, the artwork museum-worthy. I couldn't imagine what all that cost. It was mind-blowing.

I texted back.

ARE YOU CARESSING THE CABINETS?

OF COURSE. I'M TRYING TO DO IT ON THE SLY, BUT I THINK KELLY'S ON TO ME. ANNABEL KEEPS PULLING ME AWAY. SHE'S SUCH A PARTY POOPER.

I giggled.

"Poppy's in her element," Marco said as he finished the last of his eggs.

"She really is. She'll remember this day for the rest of her life."

Poppy texted again.

OFF TO WALK THE PERIMETER BEFORE WE GO. I SOLEMNLY VOW TO STAY ON THE RIGHT SIDE THIS TIME. MATT'S BEEN TELLING US SOME REALLY FUN STORIES. CAN'T WAIT TO SHARE. HAVE A GREAT RIDE BACK WITH MARCO! SO EXCITED FOR YOU! XOXO

Even in her joy, Poppy was thinking about me. She was the sweetest.

My phone beeped again, this time with Summer's tone.

HOLY CRAP! POPPY JUST FILLED ME IN ON WHAT HAPPENED TO YOU GUYS. SHE SAID YOU'RE WITH MARCO. CAN'T WAIT FOR YOU TO GET BACK SO I CAN HEAR THE GORY DETAILS FIRSTHAND.

I quickly replied, letting Summer know we'd get together as

soon as possible and wishing her well with Xander.

"Sorry about that," I told Marco. "Summer just texted. She's up in Vancouver with Xander. She missed out on all the excitement."

It was only a matter of time before I would hear from Jenny. None of us would text her this early in the morning, because she was likely still asleep. She was going to be sad she hadn't been part of the action. Jenny lived for fun.

"It's not a problem. I know how close you are with your friends." Marco had been around them quite a bit the past month, as my friends were fully invested in my success at the Watering Can and often dropped by to help out. Summer was designing the logo. I couldn't wait to see it. "How about we go take a walk on the beach before we head out? I also have to call the rental company and confirm that I'll be driving the car up to Seattle."

"The beach sounds perfect. Are you thinking we'll make the trip all in one shot?" I asked casually.

He looked at me. His gaze was heated. Downright smoldering.

It took me by surprise, even though it shouldn't have. I was pretty sure I was giving off the same smolder. I was trying to at least.

I swallowed, waiting for him to answer.

"We can decide later." His voice wavered a little. "Is that okay?"

I nodded.

It was the most I could manage.

Marco paid our breakfast tab while I tried to keep my brain on task. Imagining being with him after all these years, knowing it was within my grasp, was headier than anything I'd felt in quite some time. It was right up there with my freshman-year fantasies of him taking me right there on the book counter.

My imagination was no less active now than it'd been back then.

I was fairly certain my blush had a blush.

As we exited the restaurant, he grabbed my hand as we walked to the car. Where we touched, my fingers tingled.

Who was I kidding? Everything tingled.

"I think the main beach is just up the road," he told me as we got in the car. "It should only take a few minutes to get there."

"I can't wait."

Like, I literally couldn't wait for all the things that were about to happen.

It was Christmas Day times a thousand.

CHAPTER 12

The beach was gorgeous, nearly empty since it was still early, and a little breezy because it was spring. We walked a mile or more, sometimes hand in hand. We'd both taken off our shoes and rolled up our pants, walking barefoot while we shared stories about growing up.

"Do you have siblings?" he asked as he angled his face toward the morning sun, breathing deeply. "I think you mentioned you had a brother."

"I do have a brother," I replied. "But we weren't raised together. My parents divorced when I was three. Sam lived full-time with my dad, and I lived full-time with my mom." The salty air was invigorating. "Sam lives in Denmark now. He moved there for a job a few years ago. We're not close, but recently we've been making an effort to connect more. The practice of splitting up siblings should be outlawed. I don't recommend it for anyone. It robbed us of having an immersive sibling relationship and caused a lot of ill feelings and unnecessary competitiveness. We've since forgiven our parents, but it doesn't change how we were raised. I'm happy to say my brother and I are getting better at communicating. I love him and am looking forward to having a solid relationship with him in the future."

I'd been so busy with the prep work for the shop that I hadn't talked to my brother in a few weeks. I made a mental note to reach out to him soon.

"I'm sorry you didn't get a chance to grow up together," Marco said. "I've always wished for siblings, but not being able to live with both my parents in the same household would've been extremely hard."

It had been hard, but the only thing we'd known. "We should probably head back if we want to make it to Seattle at a reasonable time," I said reluctantly. *Reasonable* meaning *after midnight* at this point. We still hadn't discussed the possibility of stopping along the way. That would come later.

Marco had informed me that he had a client meeting tomorrow afternoon, so we needed to get on the road soon.

"Yeah, that's probably a good idea."

"Are you sure you don't want to fly back?" I asked. "I can ride back with my friends, no problem."

"I'm sure," he said. "Spending time with you is a treat."

We talked about the Watering Can on the way back to the car. I was excited to get back to work at the shop. Marco had so many good ideas that I knew without a doubt the place was going to be a success. I couldn't have asked for a better teammate.

Once we arrived at the rental, he turned, surprising me as he gathered me into his arms.

I'd never wanted anything more in my entire life than to be

held by him.

And this wasn't happening in a closet. It was out in the open and for real.

His kiss was like an explosion inside my brain.

My hands wrapped around his shoulders, and I held on for dear life.

I was kissing the man of my dreams.

And it was fantastic.

Frickin' fantastic!

We didn't come up for air for quite some time. I was hazy on the details.

In my previous life, I would've stopped kissing a lot sooner, possibly before it had even started, conscious of the world around me and my ordered place inside it. Excessive PDA was not in the top hundred things I felt comfortable doing. But I'd waited more than seven long years for this, and the freedom of actually being with Marco without any strings attached—*damn* if I wasn't going to enjoy the hell out of it.

We finally came to our senses after lots of kissing.

"We should go," he said a little breathlessly. "We have a long drive ahead of us."

"Yeah," I agreed, leaning in for another kiss.

His lips were soft and full, and they fit between mine perfectly. A few mewls came out. Being connected to him felt *that* good. Kissing him might be the most joyful feeling I'd experienced in my entire life, including all the holidays I'd celebrated as a child combined. My heart felt ready to explode. It was exhilarating that we could be together out in public and didn't have to hide.

There was no dehydrated pony here. Just me and my A game.

Eventually, we separated.

My lips tingled like crazy. So did other parts of my body. It took some rearranging and deep breathing once we'd gotten into the car to settle down.

We managed to get on the road and head out of town without ripping our clothes off. That felt pretty incredible. We fell into a nice rhythm of chatting, mostly about inconsequential things like favorite TV shows, recent binges, music we liked, and favorite coffee shops and stands around Seattle. Coffee was big for Seattleites, and everyone had their favorites.

After a few hours of driving, we pulled into a gas station to fill up, get some snacks, and go to the bathroom. Poppy would be proud of our snack consumption.

My friends hadn't left Montecito yet, so we were set to arrive back in Seattle well before them. I was fine with that. I was ready to be back.

Poppy had sent more pictures, one of which included a corner of the duke and duchess's home. She and Annabel were planning to get on the road in about an hour and would spend the night on the way. I was glad they were enjoying themselves. Yasmine was going to stay for another few days. She and Matt had talked for a while, and things were looking good, according to Poppy.

Go, Yasmine!

After Marco and I had been on the road for a few more hours, I offered to drive.

He declined, but thanked me for the offer. I finally felt ready to ask him how his marriage arrangement with Yasmine had come about and how he felt now that it was over.

We definitely needed to have this discussion before we got busy between the sheets. I needed to know that he was ready to move forward.

"So…" I paused, gathering the courage. "Tell me about how you and Yasmine got together." I was trying to sound as casual as I could. "She told me a lot of it from her perspective, but I'd love to hear the story from yours."

"Sure," he replied easily. "A marriage arrangement is not something I ever thought I'd do, so when my mother asked me to consider one, it took me a while to get my brain around the idea." He flashed me a smile. I wanted to touch him. My fingers curled in anticipation. "I agreed to talk to Yasmine—not getting on board for the actual arrangement itself yet—just to make my mother happy. She'd just started chemo. I would've done almost anything she asked at that point."

"I'm sorry your mother is sick," I said. "That's hard."

He nodded. "It's been incredibly difficult, but she's doing much better, thankfully. The tumor was in her liver, but the doctor was able to get it all, and it hadn't metastasized. The liver has the wonderful ability to regenerate, so we're hopeful." He adjusted his hands on the wheel, seeming completely at ease. "When she broached the subject of an arranged marriage with me over a year ago, I wasn't having any luck in the relationship department, so I decided why not make her happy and, at the same time, maybe find the right woman for me."

"Sounds logical," I said.

"My mother has a complicated past," he went on. "She's been estranged from her family for a very long time, and it's been incredibly painful for her. She immigrated to Spain from Morocco in the mideighties at seventeen and married my father a year later, without her family's consent. She was basically disowned after that. Then she and my father immigrated to the

US in the nineties and had me. She had a rough pregnancy with me, so I'm an only child. Her parents both died before she could return to Spain to try to make amends."

That was so sad.

It made total sense that he wanted to make his mother happy.

"We learned about Yasmine when my grandmother's best friend found out about my mom's cancer and started emailing her. She mentioned she had an eligible granddaughter who might be a good match for me. Arranged marriages are very common in Morocco, especially in the smaller villages. My mom's mother found love in her arranged marriage. And my mother has known couples throughout her life who thrived and some who didn't." He reached out to grab my hand. I smiled. "Yasmine and I started corresponding soon after. We got along so well that a few months later, it actually seemed like it might work. You've spent time with her, so you know she's nice, super smart, and has a great sense of humor. We have a lot of things in common."

"That's what she said. She said you were both very hopeful it would become a love match."

"We definitely were. Kind of our own Moroccan-American love story. We kept joking that it would be a fun tale to tell our kids one day." He ran a hand through his hair. "But after a while, the relationship just…plateaued. We didn't start to dislike each other, but it never went to the next level. Our personalities didn't mesh romantically no matter how hard we tried. She'd want to go out when I wanted to stay in, and vice versa. Our humor is different. I'm nerdy and more of an introvert. She's very extroverted. I've been in the car with you for a few hours, and every single second of it has been fluid and easy. It's never like that between Yasmine and me. There's always a barrier between us, like something is in the way. We couldn't get past it."

"You think it's because she still has feelings for Matt? This is going to sound a little strange, but I've had trouble not comparing the few men I've dated to you." It'd likely been why those unions hadn't worked out. "Or I'd compare the relationship that I imagined we would have had if we'd dated in college. I know that sounds weird, but it's true."

"I think something like that definitely played a part for her," Marco said. "Yasmine didn't tell me about Matt until just a few months ago. After I proposed and the gravity of what we were doing sank in, we both knew it wasn't the right choice. We'd become good friends, but that wasn't enough to translate into a committed marriage. She confessed her lingering feelings for Matt and told me how their breakup was weighing on her. I told her that I'd once had those feelings for someone as well, though we'd never dated. At the time, I didn't tell her it was you. But I think she figured it out when you and I went into business together and started spending a lot of time together. She actually encouraged me to invest with you, so I know, on some level, she knew it was you all along."

"I really can't believe you had feelings for me this entire time. It's like my greatest dream has become a reality."

He grinned. "You're talking to a guy who doesn't do deep dives into his emotions very often. That's why Yasmine and I stayed together as long as we did. But the way I felt when I first met you, then when I saw you again at the bank last year, is something I've never had with anyone else. This excitement wells in my chest and makes my knees feel weak." He rubbed his chest, and I'd never wanted to take a bite of anything more. "I didn't think I'd see you again after college, so I wasn't actively imagining us being together. But yes, that feeling is what both Yasmine and I agreed we wanted to hold out for. Then, when I began to have feelings for you again, I told Yasmine pretty much immediately. She told me that while we were discussing it, she realized that was exactly what she had with Matt."

"I'm so glad you guys figured that out. Have you dated other women seriously? Before Yasmine?" I'd never really asked him that before.

"Not many. And none of them made me feel especially weak-kneed. It wasn't until a few years into college that I had my first actual girl encounter," he admitted. "That sounds lame, I know. But it's true. I was dragged to a party and ended up having a few drinks. I hadn't imbibed much before then. I got a little tipsy and made out with a girl. I didn't date her or anything, but I found out that kissing a girl was a very pleasant experience." He chuckled. "Shortly after that, I got the courage up to ask out the sister of a friend. Caroline was as nerdy as I was, so I felt less intimidated. We dated for almost a year. I still keep in touch with her. She's in a long-term relationship with a woman now. We were each other's first, and I joke that sex with me ruined men for her."

I giggled.

Just thinking about having sex with this man made me giddy all over.

"She maintains the sex wasn't all that bad, but she needed to be with me to figure out she didn't want to be with men." He appeared wistful. "It's safe to say I've never been a slayer. I dated two women after that. One was extremely high maintenance. I was never able to please her, no matter how hard I tried. It was exhausting. The next one didn't want to settle down. In fact, I think she's hiking the Himalayas right now. Neither of them was a love match."

It was sweet he was sharing so much with me. "We've dated the same amount," I told him. "I've been in three serious relationships. I had a couple of high school romances before that, but I never got hot and heavy with them. My first college boyfriend was Brandon. We dated for a couple of years. He was fine, but we didn't share many interests. He was an avid sports fan, bordering on fanatic. He was a good guy, but he never wanted to do the same things or go to the same places as I did. Nobody was surprised when we broke up. Next was Tate. He was a fellow accountant. And when I tell you two accountants should not get together, it's the truth. We were the most boring couple ever. Complete homebodies. Again, he was really sweet. He just didn't do it for me. Next was Lucas. He was the most fun and spontaneous, but I couldn't match his energy. He was always busy, always moving from place to place. He wore me out, and I was worried if I stayed with him, we'd never be in the same location for longer than a year or two. I love it here. This is my home." I debated whether to say the next thing, but I went for it. "To be honest, the reason they also didn't work was that none of them were you." He met my gaze. I looked away. "I feel like admitting this to you might put extra pressure on our budding relationship, but please believe that I'm not expecting our relationship to be perfect. Don't think that. Or even some kind of ideal. We may or may not work out. But I'm so incredibly happy we get the chance to explore that together."

He reached out and took my hand. "So am I."

Then he brought my hand to his lips.

Chapter 13

I woke when the car stopped, and the engine went quiet. "Where are we?" I struggled to find the seat latch to pop me back up into a sitting position. "I was supposed to take the next shift." I wiped my eyes, blinking a few times. "Are we in Washington?"

It felt like I'd been asleep for a long time. I was very groggy.

"I couldn't bear to wake you," Marco admitted. "You hardly got any sleep last night. Your snoring is adorable, by the way."

I glanced out the window. We were parked in front of my building. "That was so sweet of you to drive the whole way." I yawned. "I feel bad I didn't at least keep you company during the final hours. I was out for a long time."

"Don't feel bad," he said. "It was a very peaceful drive. It gave me a lot of time to think about everything that's happened over the last few weeks."

"I hope good things."

"Very good." He smiled.

I bit my lip. "Do you want to come up?" I held my breath.

I really, really wanted him to come up, but I was feeling shy. We'd had several kissing sessions throughout the day—each stop for gas had been an *event*—and they'd been wonderful. I felt like those kisses had been a precursor for what was to come, what we both were craving, but so many hours had passed, I wasn't sure how he was feeling.

"I'd love to."

"Great."

We both got out and made our way into the lobby of my building and moved quietly up the stairs. Once we were both inside my apartment and I'd closed the door behind us, his hands went around my waist, and mine moved to his face.

How many times had I wanted to stroke his face like this, to touch him freely, to be near him? So many I couldn't count.

"I can't believe this is actually happening," I said.

"It's happening," he whispered, leaning forward.

I luxuriated in his full lips, teasing them, caressing them with my tongue. They were perfection. He was the best kisser I'd ever had the pleasure of kissing.

"You're amazing," he murmured, his mouth moving down my neck, his tongue leaving a cool trail. "My dream."

My thoughts were jumbled. "You're an incredible kisser." That's the first thing my scrambled brain could come up with.

"It's only because I have a very talented partner. Should we"—he indicated with a nod—"head back to your room?"

"Yes." I wanted nothing more.

We stopped in the hallway. It was a very short corridor, but I just couldn't wait. I reached up to unbutton his shirt, my hands shaking slightly. Only the ambient light from my living room lit up the space, but it was enough. His chest was magnificent. My fingertips fluttered over the hard ridges, his nipples hardening as he shivered.

A soft moan came from his lips as I bent forward and took a nipple between my teeth, flicking it with my tongue.

I'd dreamed about this.

Tasting him and licking his chest had been at the top of my list. I couldn't believe I was finally checking that off. *I was licking Marco!* My freshman-in-college self was having an absolute fit. She was literally doing jetés in my mind. I was a former dancer, and I loved expressing myself by running and leaping. It made me feel incredibly free.

His hands slipped under my shirt, his thumbs gliding over my bra, teasing me, taunting me in the same place. My toes curled from the pleasure, especially from what was about to come

I grabbed his hand and guided him into my bedroom.

He sat at the edge of my bed, and I stepped between his legs, sliding the shirt off his shoulders, watching it pool onto the bed as he slipped his arms out, his warmth seeping into my every pore. He drew me toward him, his hands grasping my sides. He undid the button on my jeans slowly, sliding them around my hips.

Once they were off, I tumbled into the bed with him, feeling like I'd won the friggin' lottery.

I won!

Our kissing was frantic. We finished undressing each other as quickly as we could, our lips barely parting.

His fingers found my wetness, and he circled with intent. I

gasped. Everything felt so good. I was more than ready. "Do you have protection?" I murmured into his mouth. "If not, I have some in that drawer." I indicated my bedside table.

It was always good to be prepared.

He rolled over and opened the drawer, getting out a condom.

As he moved and flexed, I skimmed my hands from his tight abs up to his bronzed pecs and back again. He was a feast, and I was about to sample the main course.

He turned back toward me and caressed my face, his thumb running over my bottom lip. "You know, we can wait if you want to. I don't want you to feel any pressure. I'm enjoying myself. Things happened tonight…rather quickly, and I won't feel bad if we decide to wait."

I responded by kissing him, my tongue intertwining with his, my hands raking through his hair.

After a few beautiful, breathless minutes, I replied, "I've been waiting for you for seven and a half years. I'm not waiting a second longer."

He groaned as he tore open the condom. I worked my tongue down his abs, nipping him right below his belly button, watching him roll on the condom.

His chest wasn't the only thing that was delicious.

He positioned himself over me. My hips arched toward him greedily. As he entered me, my legs wound around his waist like they had a mind of their own.

The moment he was fully inside me, we both groaned.

He stopped moving, his head bowed.

I brought my hands up to his face. I loved touching him there. His eyelids slid shut. "I've wanted this for so long," he whispered as he began slowly moving back and forth. "You feel unbelievably sweet. My young, nerdy self can't believe his luck."

I gave a throaty laugh. "Young me is living out her wildest fantasy. We make a good team." Every coil inside my body was poised to spring as he languidly stroked in and out. "I've... wanted this since the day I met you." I could barely get the words out.

He chuckled. It came out hoarse. Hearing that made my toes tingle. "Yes, but the me back then and the me now are two completely different people. I'm afraid your satisfaction wouldn t have been at the top of my list when I was a freshman in college." He punctuated his statement with a hard thrust, followed by firm, upward pressure. He lingered there for a second, allowing me to enjoy it.

I grabbed his ass, grinding into him like it was an instinct I hadn't known had been lurking inside me all along. I was pretty sure the word *wanton* had come directly from an interlude like this. I'd never felt more wanton in my life. Everything about him made my body sing. It was pure magic.

He began a faster rhythm, hitting me in exactly the right place. "Let me know if—"

"*Ohhhhh*," I moaned. "It's...perfect."

He nipped my shoulder, keeping up the rhythm as his hand slid between us, his thumb landing on my most sensitive area.

My hips bucked as my hands grasped his biceps, my nails digging in.

"Break for me," he whispered.

Hearing his sexy voice and knowing its intent sent me over the edge.

I came hard and fast.

He immediately pinned me to the bed, letting me ride out

my pleasure. He was so in tune with my body that it felt like we were of one mind.

After I came back to earth, he settled a kiss on my forehead and began his smooth rhythm again, withdrawing almost completely each time. It was fantastic.

He moved faster and faster, until I broke again, grabbing on to his shoulders. A moment later, he called out my name, his thrusts punctuated by his release.

I finally opened my eyes. Marco was panting. His hair was slicked back with sweat. He was flushed, his neck muscles corded and his pecs flexed.

He was a *sight.*

I moved against him, my hips circling, enjoying the delicious sparks and zaps of current still sizzling between us.

Once he caught his breath, he settled himself lightly on top of me. My arms reached around his broad shoulders, my fingertips fluttering over his lower back, enjoying the feeling of him. "That was…wonderful," I murmured. "I feel wrung out in the best way possible."

Without answering, he rolled us onto our sides, wrapping me up in a close embrace. My cheek pressed against his damp chest, my ear picking up his thundering heartbeats. He hadn't been able to speak yet.

He inhaled and exhaled a couple of times. "You… That… was amazing." A few more breaths. "I feel like I might've blacked out there for a minute."

I stretched out my legs, feeling exhilarated and content and just all-around fabulous. "How did you learn how to do that thing with your thumb in that position? It was amazing." I preferred men touching me the way he had during sex, but the easiest way to do that was from behind.

"To be honest, and a little cheesy," he confessed, "my workouts include one-arm push-ups for strength and balance. In my limited experience, I've learned most women prefer more than one stimulus during sex. Being the dork I am, I actually researched it." His strong, one-arm-push-up muscles flexed around me as he pressed his lips to my forehead. "Your pleasure is important to me. More so than my own."

I couldn't argue with a generous lover.

What woman in her right mind would?

"Your pleasure is also high on my list." I nuzzled his chest.

He eased me onto my back, his gaze full of intent. "Being with you was like having years of pent-up longing finally set free." He leaned down to kiss me. "I can't wait to do it again." His breath was hot in my ear.

It felt so good to be here in this moment. I'd just learned that Marco was an excellent lover. Straight-up tens across the board. I was incredibly happy. And hungry. "You want something to eat?" I asked. "We ate gas-station food for dinner what feels like forever ago."

"Eating is definitely on my mind." He licked his lips slowly.

I had to tear my eyes away so I could focus.

"Let me go see what I have. It's too late to order takeout."

Sliding out of bed, I grabbed an oversized T-shirt out of my dresser drawer and slid it over my head, then padded to my kitchen and opened the fridge.

I took out the leftover Giovanni's pizza. I chose a block of Edam cheese and was in the process of grabbing a box of crackers when Marco cleared his throat from the doorway. I hadn't heard him approach.

The sight of him standing there in just a pair of black boxer briefs took my breath away.

I was stunned into silence.

This man had chosen me.

We were finally together.

It was going to take me a long time for my brain to reconcile this development.

He moved forward, asking, "Do you need any help?"

I didn't respond. I felt like my entire life had just caught up with me.

Grinning, he wrapped his hands around my waist and lifted me onto the counter. "You look adorable standing here in your T-shirt putting a plate of cheese and crackers together." He nuzzled my neck, his lips moving from the base of my throat to the back of my ear. "You're so sexy. I'm not sure I'll ever get enough."

My hands fondled his chest. It was my current favorite thing to do. I wanted to memorize every contour. He felt so damn good. "I can tell you right now, I'm never going to get enough."

The kiss he gave me would've brought me to my knees if I'd been standing. He angled his head and delved farther, our tongues intertwining with possessive urgency.

"Do you still want to eat?" I whispered, rubbing my cheek against his chest. He smelled musky and perfect.

"Yes. It's all I can think about," he said as he lifted me off the counter.

I giggled as he walked us back to the bedroom.

He laid me on the bed gently, my T-shirt falling in a way that exposed my breasts.

He shook his head. "So beautiful."

I moved to make room for him, taking off my shirt, my hair falling around my shoulders.

He knelt on the bed, moving toward me on all fours. His gaze was so heated I thought I might burn up.

Very slowly, he spread my legs apart, his hands sliding from my knees to the insides of my thighs. "This scene playing out in my mind is what kept me awake from Oregon to Seattle," he told me, his voice barely above a whisper. "And if I don't taste you right now, I might perish."

His head bobbed between my legs, and I finally knew what heaven felt like.

Chapter 14

We haven't seen you for weeks," Poppy complained from my phone screen. "Surely you can spare a moment of your time to inform me about what's happening in your life."

I laughed. "We literally text forty-seven times a day. You know exactly what I'm up to at all times." I stood in the storage room of the Watering Can, waiting for our flower refrigerators to arrive. We'd ordered four, and I was excited to get them installed.

"That's not the same as *seeing* you," Poppy argued. "Yasmine is all moved into her new place. Summer's freaking out about her new client, which is a major brand, which is super exciting. Annabel has a new girlfriend that she's head over heels about, and you're missing in action."

"I'm not missing," I insisted. "The timing just hasn't worked out. And stop being so dramatic. We saw each other last week for coffee."

"For, like, five minutes."

I chuckled. "It can't be helped. I've been super busy setting up the shop and working with my accounting clients. Not to mention, Marco and I are in that honeymoon dating phase, and it's been a little"—I winked—"time-consuming."

"Yes, I'm well aware that Marco has a magical penis."

I sputtered, which turned into a bark of laughter. "Well, then, see? You already know everything that's happening with me." I hadn't told her about Marco's penis at all, but she had correctly inferred.

The last month together had been absolutely incredible. We'd hardly spent any time apart.

"I'm not taking no for an answer. I want to see your beautiful face in person for more than five minutes. How about tonight after work for drinks at the Driftwood? It's a few blocks from you. Surely you can muster up the energy to walk there to meet your very best friend in the whole entire world."

"I can't tonight," I told her. "Marco's surprising me with a mystery date. He's picking me up at four, and I have no clue where we're going."

"Fine." I could hear the grumble under her voice. "Lunch tomorrow, then?"

"That should work."

"Great. How about Torino's? It's in Ballard. I'll come to you. That way, you can't wiggle out."

"Perfect. How's it going with Leo?" I wandered to the front of the shop, sitting on a stool behind our newly installed counter, which was also a refrigerated cooler that would hold houseplants, ready-to-go arrangements, boutonnieres, and corsages. Our handyman had installed floating shelves that looked amazing. I'd thrifted two wooden tables that I'd painstakingly sanded and coated with oil to serve as displays for merch. They looked fabulous.

Everything was coming together.

"Crappy," she replied. It came out as a harrumph. "He's still completely distracted. Always on his phone. I have no idea what he's up to. I hint around about it, trying to fish out some information, but we don't know each other well enough for me to launch into a full inquisition. Plus, I'm still really into him, so I don't want to turn him off by being a Nosy Nicole when he obviously doesn't want to share."

"Have you asked Xander about it? They're best friends after all."

"Yeah, Summer's been acting as my intermediary. But so far, she's found out zero things. The grand opening of Zoe's Lager is two months away, and I'm really hoping we're a couple by then. The man is still a sexy beast to me, and I totally want to be with him. Those few times when he's engaged with me, and not on his phone or glancing over his shoulder, he seems totally into me. The flirting is outrageous. But honestly, it could just be my imagination at this point. Cross your fingers that the tide changes soon."

"They are totally crossed," I said, holding up my free hand to show her.

It'd taken Poppy a long time to recover from her breakup with Michael. She deserved to have a new relationship she was excited about. I was rooting for her and Leo to work out.

"Tell me about Annabel's new girlfriend." I'd seen Poppy and Summer a few times separately since we'd gotten back from our wild road trip. But I hadn't seen Annabel yet. She'd found a full-time job and had been apartment hunting fairly seriously.

"Her name is Stephanie, and she's a six-foot-tall semipro Amazonian volleyball player who's utterly gorgeous. Like, stunningly attractive. She has this long, beautiful, wavy, chestnut hair." Poppy gave her head a shake, mimicking the waves with her fingers. "Leave it to my knockout sister to date a knockout. I barely ever see her anymore, but I'm so happy for them. They seem over the moon. That is, when they come up for air. Kind of like yourself."

I giggled. "I'm not that bad."

"I beg to differ. It's 'Marco this,' 'Marco that,' 'last night I had twenty-five orgasms,' 'he leaves me love notes all over the house,' 'he bakes me cakes,' 'he sings me lullabies,' 'he gives me full head-to-toe massages each and every night.'"

"I've literally never said any of that." I laughed.

She swished a hand. "It's all implied."

"I'm very happy"—so, so happy—"and I guess that's leaking through. And if I were counting, I have had quite a few orgasms. No cakes. No lullabies. But his sexy talk is to die for. He says things to me he'd never say outside of the bedroom, and they make my toes curl, among other things. Speaking of feet, I've been on the receiving end of a couple of foot massages and a few shoulder rubs, but now you got me thinking a full-body massage is in order."

"Aww." Poppy mocked wiping a tear from the corner of her eye. "Your happiness *is* leaking through, and I'm so here for it. I'm lapping it all up. You've waited so long for this. I know I'm just being a big grouch insisting you come and see us in the flesh, interrupting your happy fun time with Marco, but I miss you."

"I miss you, too," I told her, meaning it. "It's not my intention to be out of commission. The shop is taking up a huge chunk of my time—the time I used to have for long lunches and to stop work early for happy hour." I'd known it would. Investing in my dream was hard work, but extremely fulfilling. "I've had to rearrange my schedule and slim down my client list, which has been a little stressful. Some of my accounting clients aren't too happy with me, but it was necessary, as I was starting to fall behind. I've just had a ton going on lately."

"Have you met Marco's parents?" she asked.

"No. He keeps saying soon, but it hasn't happened yet."

"Yasmine says her parents have taken their split pretty well, as far as she's shared. It hasn't been completely smooth, but they're working through it. She and Matt are not fully back together, but they're talking a lot. She seems to be in a really good place."

"That's wonderful. I can't wait to catch up." I'd seen Yasmine only twice since the trip, once when we'd gone out for coffee after she'd arrived back in town from Montecito. She'd wanted to thank me for going with her and to tell me what was happening with Matt. When she'd stayed down there for a few more days, they'd had some long talks, but they hadn't gotten intimate. She'd wanted to wait until they'd worked through all of the emotional stuff between them so the physical stuff wouldn't override everything else. It was smart, but I knew it was hard for her to wait. Then I'd seen her when she'd moved out of Marco's apartment. She'd been sweet, gracious, and seemed genuinely happy for us.

She was quickly becoming a fast friend to all of us. She and Poppy had developed an especially close bond, which didn't surprise me. They really complemented each other nicely.

"You are busy, and I promise not to hound you too much in the future. Have fun on your mystery date," Poppy said. "Oh, and try not to have too much sex."

"You can never have too much sex," I told her.

She raised an eyebrow. "You'd be surprised. After a while, the chafing gets to you."

I giggled. "I'll be sure to stock up on lube."

"Take it from a girl who knows." She made kissy lips along with a loud smack. "See you tomorrow."

"Can't wait."

"Not even a teensy clue?" I asked Marco for the second time. We were in his car. It looked like we were headed into downtown, but I wasn't sure. "Why did I have to bring a raincoat when, miraculously, it doesn't look like rain?"

"Because one can never be too sure," he replied cagily.

"Too sure about what? Bungee jumping? Rock climbing?"

He laughed. It was a wonderful sound, throaty and deep. I loved hearing it each and every time. "None of those, but if you're into that kind of stuff, I'll make a note of it in here." He tapped the side of his head.

"Maybe the rock climbing, but definitely not the bungee jumping. The thought of leaping off a cliff makes me queasy."

"Good. Me, too. I couldn't do a jump either. I can't imagine I'd be good at climbing, but that said, I'm certainly willing to give it a try."

"Honestly, heading up to Rainier on a trail is about as close as I want to get to rock climbing," I said. "The skyline loop is my favorite."

"You can't beat those views."

"You really can't. We'll have to go as soon as it warms up a little bit. I'm kind of a baby about the cold."

"I knew that." He grinned. "You actually shared your distaste of the cold at a football game once, the same game where I wore my new sweatshirt. You found me in the stands and came over to say hello. You were bundled up in not one, but two sweatshirts, gloves, and a pair of really cute pink earmuffs. I've never forgotten it. Your lips were a little blue, and I had a desperate urge to kiss them. I wanted to keep you warm, being the Good Samaritan I was. But instead, I ran off to sit with my single friend Justin. We were still playing video games together in our dorm rooms. I was quite the Romeo."

"I remember seeing you there, wishing we were sitting side by side, holding hands. I was relieved you didn't go sit by another girl."

"Not a chance. As I told you, it took me another year until I had my first actual girl encounter," he said.

Just thinking about kissing him made me tingly all over.

I laughed. "You were late to the kissing game, but I'm glad you discovered it."

"I kept imagining she was you." He glanced at me shyly as he took an off-ramp toward downtown.

"I wish it would've been," I mused. "But maybe if we'd dated back then, we wouldn't have connected like we have now. We were both younger and inexperienced. I could imagine it not working out back then."

"I don't know about that." He was contemplative. "You're so

easy to be with. You're kind, you're funny, you're sexy as hell. Pretty much everything I've ever been looking for."

I blushed. "It's easy to say that now. But back then, our nerdy, introverted selves would've gotten in the way. We needed to mature a bit, experience other things, relationship disappointments, and real-life ups and downs. As much as I wish we would've gotten together back then, I'm glad it's happening now."

"I am, too," he said. "We're both ready."

I was *so* ready.

"Have you spoken to your parents recently?" I asked.

"Um, not…not super lately." He scratched the back of his neck. I'd noticed it was one of his tells. "I think I spoke to them sometime last week."

"Have they shared any more about how they feel about the breakup?" Marco had told his parents after Yasmine had returned from California that they were no longer engaged. He'd been very scarce on the details with me, which was a little odd. He'd said only that they'd supported his decision and needed a little more time to process the news.

"They're doing the same," he assured me. "They're sad, but they'll get through it."

"If they're still having a hard time, maybe Yasmine could speak to them? I know they were close to her and likely miss her. Knowing that the breakup was mutual and that she's doing okay could help."

"Possibly," he said. "I'll mention it to her." He made another turn, and I saw Elliott Bay laid out before us. "We're here."

Chapter 15

Marco turned into the parking lot of the Bell Harbor Marina. I gaped as I took in the docks. "We're going on a boat? You have a boat?"

"No, I don't have a boat." He chuckled. "I don't think that's a purchase I would ever splurge on. But the president of my company has one. He noticed how happy I was the other day and asked me about it." He pulled into a parking spot and turned off the car. "I told him I met somebody special, and he offered me the use of his boat. We have to have it back to the marina by seven p.m., because it's getting some scheduled maintenance done." He grinned, looking adorable. "I enthusiastically took him up on his offer."

"Wow. That was so nice of him." I paused. "I'm assuming people at work didn't know you were previously engaged?"

"No. A few of them met Yasmine over the past year and knew we were dating, but I've kept my personal life personal.

Explaining my situation was not something I was interested in doing." He grasped my hand. "But it seems people have noticed an uptick in my demeanor lately. And I'm glad they did, because I'm about to take you on a cruise around Elliott Bay." He leaned over and kissed me.

His mouth was warm and comforting and yummy and perfect.

I couldn't believe I got to kiss him whenever I wanted.

Happy, happy, joy, joy!

"Taking a special someone on a romantic boat ride," he said, "is something I've always dreamed about doing."

"I'm totally excited." I'd been out on the bay a few times, once with all my friends when we'd rented a hot-tub boat. That'd been a night to remember. But my boat rides had been few and far between. "Do you know how to captain a boat?" I asked as we got out of the car.

"Rest assured, you're safe with me." He walked around to the trunk. "I've been out on this particular boat twice with my boss. I did a fair amount of driving during that time. Then he let me borrow it for my parents' anniversary a couple years ago. When I was growing up, my aunts and uncles would visit from Spain, and we'd rent cabins at this resort a few hours away. I learned how to drive boats there. It was always the highlight of my summer, as my parents could never afford to send me away to summer camp or anything like that. The cabins were tiny and basically made of plywood." He chuckled as he grabbed a large picnic basket out of the back. "But it was fun to run around with all my cousins. Being an only child can be lonely at times."

He took my hand, guiding me out onto one of the piers. This man was utterly amazing. We stopped in front of a nice-sized boat, not too big, but not super small either. "This is *Serendipitous.* It's a forty-two-foot Prestige," Marco announced. "It's a great boat, but not too in-your-face."

Standing on the dock, I could tell it was nicely appointed in creamy off-white leather and a high-gloss wood finish. It was the nicest boat I'd seen up close. "It's very stylish."

"My boss grew up a little north of here on the water. He's had a boat pretty much his entire life." Marco helped me on board, handed me the picnic basket, and proceeded to untie everything.

Nervous excitement welled in my chest. Lending a boat was such a sweet thing to do. The fact that his boss had noticed that Marco was happy and had commented on it made me feel great.

It took a while, but Marco got everything figured out, turned on the engine, and steered us out of the marina. He looked incredibly handsome at the wheel. I snapped a few pictures on my phone.

Taking pictures of my boyfriend! La la la!

The captain's seat, along with seating for six passengers, and a generous table were semienclosed in one area under a large sunroof. Tinted windows wrapped around us in an arc. The side windows slid open to give an obstructed view of the bay. It was a little breezy, as the back was completely open, but I was warm with all my layers.

The scenery was incredible.

We puttered around, chatting about life and the shop, our favorite current topic. At the rate we were going, we'd be opening the Watering Can in a few months, likely right after Zoe's Lager opened. It was an exciting time.

"I'm going to stop here so we can enjoy the picnic." Marco

shut off the motor. It wasn't very windy, which was nice. The sun was drifting lower in the sky, and its reflection in the downtown buildings was beautiful and so romantic. "Let me grab the basket."

I'd offered to set everything up once we were on board, but Marco had refused. He leaned over to kiss me before saying, "I'll be right back."

He disappeared below and returned with a beautifully arrayed meat-and-cheese tray, a bottle of champagne, and two glasses. He set the food down, and I also saw slices of a fresh baguette and strawberries, as well as some spreads, complete with cute little knives. I was enjoying being spoiled. "Wow! This is fantastic. It looks extremely delicious."

"I m going to open this bottle outside. I don't want to spill anything in here." He stepped out the back, and I heard a loud *pop*. He came back, grinning. He poured some champagne into a glass and handed it to me. "This is the same brand we had that night at the Driftwood when I agreed to become your partner. That was truly the night that set this all into motion for us. You were so engaging, beautiful, confident, and such a pleasure to talk to. I left there a different person."

"Summer picked up on our vibe," I confessed. "That's why she pulled me into the bathroom. She saw what we didn't immediately see—or what we were denying to ourselves. I assured her I was in complete control and that our relationship would remain professional." I took a sip of champagne. He must've put it in a freezer downstairs, because it was perfectly chilled. "Turns out I was a poor judge of my own character."

"I'm eternally grateful you chose not to stay professional. And you're not a poor judge at all. You followed my lead.

Everything we did is because I initiated it, and all of us are in a better place because of it. It was the catalyst that propelled us to settle for nothing less than love. Yasmine and I are so much happier apart." He poured himself a glass and raised it to mine. We clinked edges. "Here's to our journey together."

I took a long drink, then licked my lips.

My gaze landed on Marco. I knew it was heated and hungry.

He took my mouth in an aggressive kiss. I had to put down my glass so I could touch him with both hands. my absolute favorite thing to do. I couldn't get enough.

We were lost to each other.

He was such a joy to kiss.

I'm kissing my boyfriend! Like, a lot!

After an unknown amount of time, because lust clouded all things, I came to my senses. "We should probably take a look at where we are and make sure we haven't floated off somewhere." We both still had our pants on, but our shirts were long gone, my bra being the sole survivor.

Marco nuzzled my neck. "I've been keeping an eye on things. We're fine. Not many boats are out, because it's still chilly. It's not as busy as it is in the summer." He took a drink of his champagne and made a show of rolling it around in his mouth. Then he leaned over, carefully easing back the material over my breast and settling his mouth over my nipple.

The champagne was cold and tiny fizzy bubbles popped against my skin.

"Nobody's ever tried that before," I whispered on the end of a moan.

So sexy!

Marco didn't answer, because he'd taken another mouthful

and was busy with the other one. My body was draped over the back of the seat, my bones the consistency of Jell-O. The man was thorough. One of my hands raked through his hair as the other trailed between his legs, stroking. "Are we really going to do this on somebody else's boat?" I whispered, half hoping he'd say, *Yes,* and half hoping he'd say, *Absolutely not, that would be weird.*

Would it be weird? It felt a little weird.

"Only if you want to," he murmured.

Don't make me choose!

"I absolutely want to be with you," I whispered. "There's no question." I left off any decision-making for the moment.

Truth be told, I didn't know if I could wait until we got back to shore. I was already buzzing, my release coiled and ready. All the fondling and kissing had been amazing.

After more lip play, I asked, "What does your boss think we're doing? I mean, does he think we're doing this? Like, specifically?"

"I don't think he's thinking about it one way or another. He's happily married with three kids. He knows what twentysomethings are like. I wouldn't use his bed or anything like that, but fooling around out here is perfectly fine."

"Are you sure no one can see us?" I arched my head up to peek out the window.

There was no one around. We were miles from the marina, bobbing in the water.

"Nobody can see us. The windows are tinted, and the partition protects us from somebody viewing us from the rear. But we don't have to do anything if you're not comfortable. I certainly didn't bring you out here expecting sex. I brought you out here because I wanted to share this experience with you."

I smiled, feeling shy.

Having sex in wild places wasn't something I'd done before. *Is this considered* wild? *Not really, but it feels like it to me.*

Lucas had always wanted to do it in the woods or on a beach, and I'd always refused. But if Marco asked me to do the same thing right now, I might. Who cared about twigs, and sand, and grass, and acorns, when you were with someone who made your heart burst with joy?

I guess I didn't, which was weird.

"I want to." I did.

He gathered me in his arms, our tongues intertwining. His mouth was so sweet. In five seconds flat, we were panting again. I unzipped his pants, my hands wandering. He managed to get mine undone, his fingers slipping inside. I shuddered. After a few minutes of finger play, I murmured, "Did you bring a condom?"

He drew out his wallet while I shed my pants. He tore it open and rolled it on. My mouth was back on his a moment later.

Without communicating in words, he guided me onto his lap.

I straddled him, and our lips connected furiously. I'd never loved a tongue more. As we were lost to the moment, he gently maneuvered my body around so I was facing away from him. I was surprised, but went with it.

"This way, I can touch you at the same time," he murmured, his lips trailing down my back.

The seat was wide enough for me to kneel. I slowly eased down on him, reverse-cowgirl style. I'd attempted this position once or twice, but it'd never quite been all that and a bag of chips. Mostly, the work required had outweighed the pleasure.

Once I was seated fully, I could barely contain myself.

It felt really, really good.

I started a tentative rhythm. After I knew all our parts lined up, I sped up. One of Marco's hands wrapped around my hip, moving to the front, while the other came around to my chest.

The double stimulation felt wonderful.

This might be my new favorite position.

I leaned forward, positioning myself at an angle to reach maximum G-spot efficiency. That, coupled with Marco using his fingers, and I was ready to explode. My eyes were closed, my head arched back, my hands on Marco's knees, squeezing.

My body was on fire.

"So sexy," Marco moaned, his voice thick and raspy. "I've imagined doing this with you so many times."

I could not contribute to the conversation. I was lost. As I moved faster and faster, I broke, shouting his name.

I shouted!

I literally never shout.

Marco came seconds later, securing me to him with both hands, his hips coming up off the seat as he pounded into me.

It took several moments for us to figure our brains out.

"Oh…damn," I panted. "That was…incredible."

Once I could think again, I leaned back against his chest, both of us still somehow connected. He hugged me to him. He was wet with perspiration, his hands moving up and down the length of my body.

In the distance, a motor sounded.

Marco lifted me smoothly off of him and yanked up his pants while plucking up his shirt. I grabbed for my clothes, giggling hysterically. We both dressed in under two seconds flat, pretending everything was normal and that we hadn't just had wild sex on a boat.

Outside, the boat didn't pass within sighting distance, and it was going a million miles an hour, its passengers completely ignoring us.

I slid my arm around Marco's waist, settling my head against his chest, still laughing. "I've never seen two people move that fast in my entire life. I guess we're both still a little prudish when it comes to outdoor sex."

"Hmm," he muttered into my hair. "I'm not going to argue, as I'm an unabashed rule follower, but it was totally worth it, even with the small possibility that somebody could've seen us. I'm thinking the next time we're at the skyline loop, we should find a good spot off the path—"

My lips silenced any other wild ideas. At least for right now.

Who knew what the future would hold? Although I knew it was going to involve a lot of good sex.

Yay for us!

After our intimate interlude, we ate the delicious nibbles Marco had thoughtfully brought and laughed, imagining what would've happened if we'd been caught in the act.

When the sun was a few inches from the horizon, the day edging toward dusk, we decided to head back. It took us twenty minutes to get back to the marina.

As Marco directed the boat into the slip, I moved, stationing myself in the front and leaning over the bow, ready to help secure the boat.

"Watch yourself," Marco cautioned as the large buoy-clad piling came within my grasp. I held on while he jumped out and tied the boat up.

Once he was done, I went to gather our things. We'd already cleaned everything up. In fact, we were leaving it cleaner than we'd found it. Two type-A personalities doing their best work.

Marco helped me onto the dock. I tried not to blush thinking about what his boss would think the next time he boarded this boat. Would he wonder about what we'd done? Probably not. A guy like that had enough on his mind trying to keep his portfolio comfortably in the black. Plus, Marco had said he had three kids. They took up a lot of mind space, didn't they? I chose to believe that.

I hoped I wouldn't meet this man for a long time.

Marco and I walked hand in hand back to his car, him carrying the empty picnic basket. I laid my head on his arm as we turned to watch the sun dip below the horizon.

When the sky morphed into a brilliant orange, shooting pink hues along the bottoms of the clouds, creating a spectacular sunset, I sighed. "This was the best date I've been on in a long time," I told him. *Ever? Quite possibly.* "Thank you so much for bringing me."

He kissed the top of my head. "It was perfect. Just like you."

Chapter 16

Something just feels off," I admitted to Poppy as I ran my fork through my salad. We'd met for lunch at Torino's. "I don't think he's told his parents he's dating someone new. Or, if he has, maybe they're irate. He refuses to talk about them at all. And I know from what Yasmine told us in the car on our way down to Montecito that they used to have dinner with them at least once a week. He hasn't gone over there in almost a month. I can't help but think I'm the reason he doesn't see them." I speared a crouton that promptly broke in half. "I can't be responsible for a breach in their relationship. He adores his parents. That would be horrifying."

"Maybe he's just giving them space," Poppy suggested gently. "He proposed to Yasmine and made it official, and just a short time later, they called it off. His parents are probably reeling a little bit, and he doesn't want to push it."

"I totally get that. I do. Giving them space makes sense." I gave up on my salad, setting down my fork. "But it makes me sad that he won't communicate with me about what's going on. In literally every other facet of his life, he's completely open and willing to talk, but he shuts down or changes the subject whenever I ask him about his parents."

"Have you spoken to Yasmine about it?" Poppy had gotten the pasta special, and it looked delicious, with lots of veggies in a creamy sauce.

"I haven't," I said. "She's moving on with her life, and I don't want to bother her with this."

"I don't think she would view it as a bother at all," Poppy replied. "I bet she's open to chatting about it. She'd probably have some insight about why Marco is acting the way he is."

"Yeah, maybe I'll reach out." I mulled it over.

Poppy took a bite of her pasta. "Guys aren't always on the same wavelength as us about sharing their emotions. I'm sure everything's fine. Marco is such a transparent guy, if anything bad was going on, you'd know it."

"I'm not so sure." Thinking about Marco not being truthful or having a fallout with his parents completely bummed me out. Time to take a breather from this topic. "How's the brewpub coming along?"

"Great," Poppy replied enthusiastically. "We're trucking along right on schedule. The guys decided to do booths along the side wall, and I just finalized the details yesterday. I can't wait for you to see it. I'm mixing a bunch of different styles, so it's going to be quirky and super eye-catching. I was worried for a second there it might be too much, but I don't think so at all now. It's just the right amount."

"I'm sure it's going to be amazing," I told her. "You're an

incredibly talented designer. Once Zoe's has its grand opening, I'm positive it will be the talk of the town. And Seattle is a big town. You're going to have a lot of job offers come from this."

"Man, I hope so." Poppy stabbed a mushroom. "Then at least I'll have one thing going in my favor."

"That bad with Leo, huh?" I asked.

"It's not bad, exactly," she said. "It's just not…much of anything. Most of the time, I feel like he's not interested, but then he'll do something, and I'm positive he *is* interested. We're having this weird emotional tug-of-war of will-he-or-won't-he. I should be woman enough to walk away and say enough is enough, but I really like him." She frowned, sticking her bottom lip out. "He's sweet, he's funny, he's generous, he's absolutely my type one thousand percent. I'm so attracted to him that when we're around each other, I feel like rubbing my head and face all over his body like a cat marking her territory, and then I want to ravage him while purring." She took another bite of pasta, pausing thoughtfully. "I'm sure once we're not working together every day, he'll forget about me, and that'll be that. The decision of whether or not we're going to be together will be made for me, and honestly, it will be a relief. I can't take much more of this back-and-forth. The sexual tension was cute in the beginning. Now it's agonizing."

"He's not going to forget about you." I took a sip of water. "I haven't seen the two of you together recently, but on the occasions I have, he's been absolutely into you. He pulls out your chair, he brings you a drink, he does all the things that a boyfriend does. It seems intentional and romantic."

"I know!" she exclaimed. "You'd think that would lead to the next level, but it never does." She made a face, raising her eyebrows and puckering her lips, and I giggled. "Then he whips out his phone, and he's gone. When that happens, a lot of times, he just leaves the pub without even saying goodbye. It's so weird. And hurtful. I should just tell him to go jump in a hole."

"I get it. Maybe it's time to have a chat with him? Put it all on the line."

"Egads, no!" she sputtered. "Well, not until after the opening, anyway." She speared a penne noodle. "It would be awful to have him tell me he wants nothing to do with me and then have to work side by side for the next four weeks. Blech."

"That's understandable. I lived in a place of unrequited love for a very long time. But look at me now." I spread my arms wide, and she giggled. "You'll get there. The waiting sucks, but arriving at your intended destination is amazing. I know you're going to figure it out."

"Hopefully," she lamented. "If Leo and I don't end up together, ultimately I'll be fine. Eventually. There are other fish in the sea or whatever." She spun her fork before popping a mushroom into her mouth. "I'm just sick of looking for the right partner, you know? It's hard to meet men without using an app, and now you guys are paired up and super happy. I'm ready to have that kind of relationship. I love sharing my life with someone. It's magical. I miss it. And I don't want to be left behind while you guys start planning your weddings and having babies."

"You're not going to be left behind," I assured her. "You're going to find a perfect match. Love doesn't operate on a timeline. It'll find you. And let's not get ahead of ourselves. Summer and Xander might be on a fast track, as they're already talking about living together, but I don't feel anywhere near there with

Marco. It's going to be a while before we're ready for that level of commitment, even though I've had my heart set on him for years. Relationships are complicated and messy."

She grumbled, "You should see my sister and her girlfriend. I've never seen Annabel so over the moon. Stephanie could be it for her. And Annabel's two years younger than me. Don't get me wrong. I'm ridiculously happy for them. But I want that for myself."

"You'll have it. You're a loving, caring, smart, feisty, incredibly funny catch and a half," I boasted. "If I liked women, I'd date you."

"Really?" She narrowed her eyes. "C'mon. I'm not your type."

"Why would you think that?"

"Because I can be high maintenance on occasion." She shook her finger at me. "But only on occasion. I'm a bit bossy, I irritate you to no end with my yammering, and I'm a short, nonathletic blonde. You're currently in a relationship with a tall, dark, handsome man who enjoys working out. Those things don't match. They're not even in the same stratosphere."

I chuckled. "It's what's in here that matters." I pointed to my heart.

"Yeah, tell that to down here." She gestured between her legs, and I burst out laughing. "This"—she pointed to her heart—"doesn't always stimulate this"—she made a pointed head bob downward. "But I appreciate the sentiment. I do. You always make me feel better, Evie. I love you so, even though we'll never roll around in the sack together." She took a sip of her iced tea. "I hope you get this figured out with Marco and his parents soon. I want you happy and stable so you can hold my hand when I need it. Because handholding is going to be necessary when Leo dumps me. You'll probably have to buy me ice cream and pizza, too. Let's not sell ourselves short. And I like the fancy stuff. No skimping."

"He's not dumping you," I said. "And if necessary, I will absolutely provide handholding and good, quality treats." I picked up my fork again to attempt to finish my salad. "I hope I get it figured out with Marco soon, too. If he's lying, or keeping important details from me, it's going to affect our relationship. I have a funny thing about lying, as you know."

"You do. You're a strong moral, ethical, law-abiding human being. But I don't think he's lying. And if he's keeping something from you, it's probably for a good reason. Marco strikes me as equally ethical, and if he's not being truthful, he's got a very good reason for it."

"Let's hope so."

"Did you speak to your parents today?" I asked over dinner. We were seated at the island in Marco's kitchen, having a dinner of leftovers from a Thai place we loved. Marco had gotten off work later than usual, but we'd wanted to have dinner together, so I'd waited. I was spending the night at his place tonight. Or that was the plan, anyway.

He shook his head. "I was going to, but never got around to it. I'll reach out to them tomorrow."

"Maybe we should invite them to dinner?" I shrugged, hoping I was coming off extremely casually. "We could cook something here, or take them to a restaurant. I'd love to meet them."

"Yeah, that sounds like a good idea."

"Really?"

He raised his eyebrows over his spring roll, giving me a questioning look. "Sure. I can't wait for them to meet you. But I have a feeling they're going to be busy for a while, so I don't know when we'll be able to get it on the schedule. It might be a bit."

"Busy with what?" I asked, keeping my tone light.

"Oh, um, some of their friends are coming into town."

That sounded a little off, but it could be true. I took a few more bites and pondered my next tactic. I had to get this out of my system, where it was beginning to fester. That wouldn't be good for either of us. "You know, it's okay if your parents don't want to meet me," I said. "I'm fine with that. I was actually surprised you decided to tell them we were together in the first place. We can give them as much time as they need."

Instead of answering, he got off his stool and walked to the refrigerator. He glanced over his shoulder. "Do you want a beer?"

"Sure."

He came back to the island, holding two beers. He picked up the bottle opener on the counter and popped the tops. "They totally want to meet you. We'll set it up once their friends leave." He handed me a cold one.

I took a sip and set it down. "Okay." I moved my pad Thai around on my plate. This wasn't going as well as I would've liked. "You know, it's okay if you haven't actually told them about us." I hesitated, glancing up, trying to gauge his reaction. But he wasn't looking at me. "I would totally understand. You were engaged to another woman only a few short months ago.

You said your parents were understanding when you told them you and Yasmine broke it off, but that's a lot for anyone to take in, so if you ultimately decided not to tell them about us, that's fine." Internally, I was pleading with him to tell me the truth without explicitly saying that. I was trying to give him an easy out by telling him I would forgive it all.

His phone chimed, and he picked it up. His brows furrowed for a quick second, then he set it down. He took a few hurried bites of food, then carried his plate to the sink. "I'm sorry, but I have to make a call." He came to my side and planted a kiss on my forehead. "I'm going to step outside for a few minutes. I'll be right back."

"Is everything okay?" I asked his retreating back as he walked to the door.

"Yeah, it's just my cousin Sophia. They're planning to visit from Spain next month, and she needs some recommendations of where to stay and all that."

I got off my stool, trailing after him. "When you get back, I'd love to finish our conversation."

He nodded. "For sure." He opened the door, then just as he was about to leave, he stepped back and gathered me into his arms. 'Everything's going to be fine. I promise." He kissed the top of my head.

After he left, I stared at the door for a solid minute.

Then I padded over to the counter and grabbed my phone. I typed a quick text to Yasmine.

HEY, ARE YOU FREE THIS WEEK?

I was relieved when I saw the three dots emerge instantly.

SURE. I'D LOVE TO SEE YOU. LUNCH? DRINKS?

I typed back.

ANYTHING WORKS FOR ME. HOW ABOUT TOMORROW?

Yasmine replied.

I HAVE MEETINGS ALL MORNING. DOES A LATE LUNCH WORK? TECHNICALLY, IT COULD BE EARLY DRINKS. ARE YOU GOING TO BE IN BALLARD?

I responded.

YES. I'M AT THE SHOP ALL DAY TOMORROW. WE CAN WORK AROUND YOUR SCHEDULE. JUST TEXT ME, AND WE'LL FIGURE IT OUT.

She replied.

SOUNDS GOOD. SEE YOU THEN. [SMILEY FACE EMOJI]

I set my phone down and paced to the beautiful windows with the gorgeous, unobstructed view of Elliott Bay. I couldn't help but bite my lip. I knew for certain that Marco was lying to me. I just couldn't figure out why.

I hoped I'd get to the bottom of it tomorrow.

CHAPTER 17

It's so good to see you." Yasmine tugged me into a quick embrace. Yasmine's meetings had run over, and since it was after five, we'd decided to meet for happy hour instead.

"You look absolutely incredible," I told her. "You're literally radiating sunshine."

"Do you think so?" She grinned as she sat back down. She'd been seated before I'd arrived. "I've honestly never been happier. Even though my life is a whirlpool with a constant eddy, I've never been more content. I feel like I'm finally on the path I'm supposed to be on, and it's an incredible feeling."

Our server came, and I gave her my drink order as well as an order for a basket of fries.

"That's so wonderful and exciting." I refrained from clapping a la Poppy, but I came close. "Tell me all about Matt and what's going on. I can't wait to hear all the juicy details."

"Oh my goodness." She took a sip of her mojito. "There's a

lot to catch you up on. Let's see, Matt left the bodyguard job less than a week after you met him. He'd accepted a job with the Los Angeles Police Department in the forensics department about a month before that. It's more of a paid internship, because he doesn't have all the experience needed, but he'd taken additional courses while living in Santa Barbara, so he has the right schooling. He's super excited, and it's going well. He's flown up here twice, once to help me get organized in my new apartment, and then again three days ago." She leaned forward, lowering her voice. "We haven't, you know, been *together*, together yet." She stuck her tongue in her cheek and grinned. "But I think it will happen soon. We're not in a committed relationship yet, per se, but the more we talk, the more we get resolved. We've had a lot of emotional baggage to cover, and those talks have been pretty intense." She settled a hand over her heart. "But I'm certain, more so than ever, that reconnecting with this man was the right thing to do. He's everything to me, and I'm so excited about our future. Every single day when I wake up, it's like I've been given this second chance at love, and I'm so grateful."

Our server brought over my gin and tonic and set down a basket of fries.

"I'm so incredibly happy for you. That's beyond fantastic." I squirted ketchup in the corner of the basket and dipped a fry. "You guys are totally meant to be. It's a swoon-worthy love story. How did your parents take the news of your breakup with Marco? I've heard bits and pieces from Poppy, but you and I haven't had a chance to chat about it."

She popped a fry into her mouth. "Yum. These are so good. The bar food here is actually delicious." She brought a napkin up to her lips and then set it in her lap. "My parents are doing fairly well. It was both harder than I thought it would be and easier at the same time. It was tough because their disappointment was palpable. They vacillated between being angry and sad, trying to find someone to blame. Then they launched into abject worry. When I told them I was talking to Matt again, they weren't happy, but they didn't object either. We've had several chats about it over the last month, and I think they're finally coming around. They value my happiness, and I'm grateful for that. At the same time, they want to make sure I'm *taken care of.*" She'd placed air quotes around *taken care of.* "It's such an old-school way to look at the world. I'm fully capable of taking care of myself. I have a degree, a great job. I make enough money to support myself, as well as send money home to them. But if I'm not connected to a worthy partner, none of that holds weight no matter how much I try to convince them otherwise." She took another drink of her mojito. "But as time goes on, they're beginning to see it my way. My mom actually asked me the other day what Matt's family is like. That's the first time she's brought up a question about his upbringing. I'm taking that as a win."

"That's great," I told her. "Have you…um…happened to have talked to Marco's parents lately?"

She raised her eyebrows in question. "No. Marco and I decided to tell our parents separately. Aleah and Antonio have not reached out." She picked up another fry. "I figure they will at some point. They're still likely hurt that things didn't work out between us. My parents haven't reached out to Marco either. So, not incredibly strange, considering. I'm a little sad, because I adore Aleah and Antonio. Have you met them yet? They're incredible people. Loving, sweet, generous. I could go on and on. They're going to be amazing in-laws and even better grandparents. They are going to spoil your kids rotten." She glanced at me, her mouth forming a small O. "I'm sorry. Do you want kids? That was a little insensitive of me. I should've asked first."

"Yes, I want kids," I replied. "Not insensitive at all. I can't wait to be a mom. But I haven't met Marco's parents, and that's part of why I wanted to get together with you. Not that I didn't want to hear everything that's going on with you, because I totally did. I'm extremely excited that everything is working out between you and Matt. But Marco's been acting a little weird lately, and I was hoping you'd have some advice or possibly even some answers."

"Weird how?"

"Actually…" It was hard to articulate what I meant without feeling a little foolish. "I think he might be keeping the truth from me or bending it a little bit. It took me a while to figure out that he hasn't been speaking about his parents, and he hasn't gone to see them lately. The night you guys decided to tell your respective parents, he told me that his took the news well. He seemed upbeat. He also said he told them he was dating me, which was a surprise. We'd talked ahead of time about him omitting that part to give them some room to get used to the idea that you guys were breaking up." I picked up my gin and tonic. "Then, after that, he sort of refused to talk about it. I've been bringing it up more often on purpose, but he just dodges my questions. Last night, I told him we should invite them over for dinner, and he said that sounded like a good idea. I was relieved. But when we talked further, he told me that they were busy with friends and didn't know when they'd be able to work it into their schedule." I took a sip of my drink. I was full of restless energy. I set the glass down, folding my arms on the table. "Then he got a text from his cousin Sophia during dinner and pretty much ran out of the apartment to call her. When he came back, he said he had some work he had to finish and pulled out his laptop. I ended up heading back to my apartment, because I didn't want to make everything into a huge deal. But something feels off, and I'm going to be so heartbroken if he's lying to me."

"Wow, that's strange. That doesn't sound like Marco at all. He's honest to a fault. He's the most trustworthy guy I've ever met. I can't imagine him lying about something like this."

"I know. That's one of the reasons I care about him so much. He's a heart-on-his-sleeve kind of guy. I adore his integrity. So, none of this is making sense, and I need it to make sense."

"I don't blame you."

"After you guys each told your parents about the breakup, I know you chatted. Did he say anything then? Something about his parents being upset? I'm looking for anything to clear this up."

Yasmine shook her head. "No, nothing in particular. It sounds like I got the same information you did. It was a pretty brief conversation. We were both incredibly relieved that it was over. We hugged and vowed to remain best friends for life. We laughed about the fact that we stayed together much too long, reminisced about the journey, and wished each other well. We haven't seen each other much since, only texting here and there. We've both been busy with work and life. Now that you mention it, it's a little weird that he didn't talk to me more about their reaction." She dipped a fry. "A few nights later, after our initial big talk, my parents video-chatted me, and I shared what they'd said with Marco as I was packing my things up in the apartment, just their concerns and their angst, but he didn't offer anything up on his side." Our server came back, and we ordered a few more nibbles. "I've been in my own head since then, so I haven't been tuned in to what's going on with him."

"Do you think his parents may have disowned him for breaking the contract, or something like that?" I asked. "I know that's jumping to a huge conclusion. But I feel like it has to be something big if he's avoiding it so hard. He wouldn't risk lying if it wasn't something life-changing." I had to believe that.

"I agree. It would have to be a pretty big deal for him to omit the truth, but I don't see that happening. Marco is their only son, and they absolutely adore him. 'Doting' doesn't even come close to describe it. They full-on slather him with love, painting it on with a thick brush. He could probably marry a mannequin, and they'd come around eventually. So, no, I don't think they would disown him."

"What else could it be? I'm genuinely perplexed. I even gave him an out last night, telling him that if he hadn't actually told his parents we were dating, I was fine with it. His response was to get up and grab a beer, and then his phone beeped." I ran a hand through my hair. It was hard not to feel flustered. "This entire thing is throwing me for a loop, and I know if I don't deal with it soon, it's going to affect our relationship negatively, and I don't want that. We've been so happy together these past few weeks. But whatever this is, it's proving to be a stalemate. The only thing left to do is confront him about it. But if I do, I feel like it could backfire, because there has to be a genuine reason for his refusal to talk, right? Something bigger than the two of us. So confronting him could trigger something we can't take back." I didn't want to risk it without good reason.

"Before you speak to him, let me poke around and see what I can find. Our parents all know each other, so I can likely convince my mom to reach out, or possibly my grandmother. We'll get to the bottom of it." She swirled her straw. "This is very out of character for the Marco I know. But I'm sure there's a logical reason why he's avoiding your questions. I'd stake my life on it. He's not an overly emotional guy, so he's probably not reading into it like you are. He also loathes hurting someone's feelings. So my guess is either he's worried about his parents' feelings or yours, or both, and he doesn't want to upset anyone. He probably thinks he can handle whatever this is on his own or resolve it at a later date. Either way, we'll get to the bottom of it." She flashed me a genuine smile and patted my hand.

"Thank you so much for helping me. I appreciate it," I told her, feeling immense relief. "I didn't want to bother you with this. You're sitting across from me radiating sunshine, and your life is on this brand-new sparkly path. Pulling you back into all this was not my intention. But you know Marco so well, better than anyone else. It's comforting to me that you guys are still friends. I'm so glad your relationship remined intact."

"I am, too. And it's not a bother at all. I'm very invested in the two of you making it work. Nothing would make me happier than Marco getting his happy ending with such an amazing woman."

I blushed. "That's so nice of you to say. I don't deserve that."

"You totally do. You're such a great match for him. You're caring and generous, and you two share the same likes and hobbies. The Watering Can is going to be a smashing success. It all fits. I'm not sure I was a believer in fate before, but I'm edging that way. It helps that I was already a proponent of things happening for a reason. I was with Marco for a reason, you guys went into business together for a reason, we're sitting across from one another for a reason." She placed her hand over mine. "I'm sure it's going to work out. I can feel it in my bones. Relationships are complicated, especially in the beginning when two people are getting familiar with each other. Marco doesn't know what you can and can't handle yet. I'd bet my skinny bank account that he's terrified of upsetting you and of the possibility of losing you. He's probably trying to protect you so you won't get hurt."

"Yeah, but hurt by what?" I asked. "That's what's scaring me. The only thing I can think of is that his parents are angry and are going to try to make him choose them or me. I couldn't bear it if he no longer had a relationship with them. I'm distant from my own brother because we didn't grow up in the same household. Communicating and keeping up with each other takes a lot of work. I'm barely in contact with my father. The way my parents chose to bring us up was a travesty. Marco has a wonderful, loving relationship with his parents. From my point of view, that's a gift and a blessing. I couldn't possibly stand in the way of that."

"I don't think you'll have to. I really don't. It has to be something else."

"I hope you're right," I said. "I'm just really anxious to figure it out and move forward. It feels like there's a logjam in the relationship suddenly. I know he feels it, too, but doesn't want to address it. I'm trying to respect that, but as my anxiety increases, it's getting harder and harder."

"Marco is an amazing man. Don't forget that. Whatever this

is, there's going to be a good explanation for it. And, honestly, if there's not, he's fooled both of us. And that's not an easy task. We're both smart, savvy, highly intuitive women. Marco Cruz is not a sociopath capable of hoodwinking us." We giggled. Nothing could be further from the truth. "So rest easy, we'll figure it out together. I'm here for you."

I felt like reaching across the table to give her a hug. Instead, I raised my drink, and we clinked glasses. "You're the absolute best."

Chapter 18

Do you really think he's lying to you?" Summer asked as she prepared tea for us.

I sat on Summer's love seat. We were meeting to go over the logo she'd created for the Watering Can. "Not exactly lying." I mean, omitting the truth *was* lying, but this felt less intentional. "More like avoiding. He won't answer my questions about his parents. Something is definitely going on, and Yasmine confirmed last night that his behavior is odd. She doesn't think this is typical for him either, which I already knew. She texted me this morning that she's talking to her mother later today. She's going to try to have one of her family members reach out to Marco's parents and poke around for information."

Summer carried the tea over, handing me a mug. She took a seat in her sunny-yellow rocking chair. "That's so strange. It doesn't sound like Marco at all. Did you end up talking with him after you went out with Yasmine?"

I took a sip of the lemon chamomile tea. Very nice and soothing. "No. We texted a little bit. He invited me over, but I declined. I'm a little nervous to see him, because I don't want this to morph into a huge deal." I cupped my hands around the warm mug. "Our relationship is new and fragile. But if Yasmine doesn't get information soon, I will absolutely confront him about it. I'll have no other choice."

Confrontation was one of my least favorite things to do in life. Not only did it make me anxious, it gave me heart palpitations. Just thinking about it now made me begin to perspire.

"What do you think he's keeping from you? Like, he didn't actually tell his parents he and Yasmine broke it off? Or that they did, and they're angry about it?"

"Something like that." I considered what I thought was the most likely scenario. "My guess is that he told them the engagement was off, and that upset them, and then he told them he was already dating something new, and they couldn't handle that. Some drama like that. More than likely, he's just worried about hurting my feelings. And I totally get that! Don't get me wrong, I do. But the whole not knowing is way worse than him telling me he lied to spare my feelings. Not to mention, if his parents are angry, he'll be forced to choose between us, at least for the time being. That would be awful. I honestly didn't want to be melodramatic about it, but here I am being exactly that. I'm so excited to be with this man. I don't want anything to go wrong, which I know is compounding the situation. Maybe I'm too hypersensitive about wanting it all to be perfect right from the get-go. No relationship is perfect." I drank some more delicious tea. "I'm probably just being silly, and it's nothing." It didn't feel like nothing, but it certainly could be a much smaller issue than I was making it out to be.

Maybe his parents were actually fine with everything, but just wanted some space to process it all, and he didn't want to talk about it until they were ready.

Summer tucked her feet underneath her. It was sunny outside, and her loft was bright and cheery. It was such a cute setup, eclectic and mismatched. It suited her perfectly. "I don't think you're being silly at all. His behavior is giving you a red-flag vibe, so you have no choice but to listen and investigate. Once you get to the bottom of it, things will go back to normal. I'm sure of it."

"I've lusted after this man for so long." I slumped back into the pillows. "On the pedestal I created in my mind all those years ago, this man is pure perfection. I'm having trouble reconciling the fictitious Marco my brain conjured up with the real Marco. That might be the root of all this. Blending them into one real human who has flaws has been difficult. When you've idolized somebody for as long as I have, and they don't live up to your expectations, where do you go from there? You cry on your girlfriends' shoulders, that's what you do. Just listening to myself telling you all this feels pathetic."

"You're not crying, and you're anything but pathetic," she consoled. "Eve, your feelings are legitimate. In the past, your boyfriends have mostly been nice and proper. Marco is an emotional choice for you, so you're invested in a different way. Your heart is on the line this time. He gets your blood pumping in a way the others didn't. Kind of like Xander and me." She winked. "It's the only kind of relationship I recommend these days, by the way. Go for the guy who gives you all the feels. Who knew you and I were each dating guys in the past who weren't fulfilling us because we were scared to take an emotional plunge? Well, you weren't scared," she corrected. "You were just biding your time, waiting for an opening. I was the one who was scared."

"You're right about the emotional part. My feelings are off the charts with Marco. But 'nice and proper'?" I chortled. "What does that even mean? All my past boyfriends were fun and social." That was the truth. "They had stable jobs, if that's what you mean by 'proper.'"

Except Lucas. He'd been in the process of getting his real estate license when I'd met him. I had no idea if he was still doing that, or if he'd gone in a different direction, but he'd been my most flamboyant pick, if *flamboyant* could refer to a man who changed jobs every three years or so.

Summer giggled. "It wasn't meant as a burn. You've just been very thoughtful about your relationships. You've picked really good guys who are steady and easygoing. You seemed happy when you were with them. But being with Marco is different. In a good way. He brings out an unstable side of you. You're not as rule-followy when you're around him. I've noticed a difference in your behavior. You're more"—she swung both hands in circles in front of her—"caught up in the moment. Does that make sense? Again, not a burn. Just facts."

She was right.

I did feel a little out of control when I was around him, and this was literally the only time I'd ever felt like that in a relationship. I didn't hate it, which was weird. In fact, I felt the exact opposite. I found myself craving that feeling.

And I *had* been happy with my boyfriends in the past. But there was a difference between being happy and being fulfilled.

Summer was right. It seemed I'd picked nice, proper guys in the past.

It wasn't that Marco wasn't both of those things. He was just *more.* I guess it shouldn't have been surprising that loving him might be more complicated.

I drank some more tea and contemplated what she'd said. "I'm not sure how I feel about being less rule-followy, since I enjoy rules." I really did. Order in the world just made sense. "Which might explain why I'm having such a hard time with this. Things should go in their proper place. People should act predictably. When they don't, it causes my anxiety to skyrocket." I rubbed the back of my neck. I felt like I was getting rashy having this discussion. "I really want this to be solved so we can move on and grow closer. I want our relationship to progress without feeling like there's a hurdle we can't jump over." I shook my head, my gaze landing on Summer's big front window. "It doesn't feel insurmountable, but if it keeps going, it will be. I don't want to back him into a corner or try to catch him in a lie. I just literally want to know what's happening with his parents. Then I want to help him figure it out."

"You'll get that chance," she told me. "This man is incredibly crazy about you. From what you've told me and what you guys discussed about your road trip with Yasmine, he's been into you for a long time. Maybe just as long as you've been into him. He was in an arrangement in which he was on track to marry a woman he wasn't crazy in love with. And suddenly"—she snapped her fingers—"he's with the woman of his dreams. Or at least a woman he's been thinking about for a long time. There's no doubt that that kind of realization could throw him for a loop, make his decision-making a little less solid. If he thinks for a second he's at risk of losing you, it might make sense that he'd react cautiously. He's not going to put your relationship in jeopardy if he can help it. Now, if whatever's going on happened a couple years into the relationship, then it might be a betrayal. This? This feels like a man who's willing to sacrifice a lot to make sure there are no early bumps in the relationship."

"Yasmine said just about the same thing."

"See?" Summer was upbeat. "This is already getting solved. Whatever is going on with Marco, he's trying to deal with it without worrying you. That's my take, anyway."

"I hope you're right."

"You're in the throes of a budding relationship. Remember how I reacted when Stacy confronted me and told me she was Xander's fiancée? I was overly emotional. I wasn't thinking straight. I was caught up in this crazy love hurricane between Xander and me, and I thought the world had stopped on its axis because he'd lied to me. I should've called Xander right then and there and asked him to explain, trusting that everything he'd said to me the short time we'd been together was the truth and not a lie. But I didn't. Instead, I ran home crying. We each come to a relationship with our own baggage and trauma. Whether it's from previous boyfriends, family, broken female relationships, everything is up for grabs. Marco's behavior is obviously triggering you, and that's fine. But take it from me— go into this with a calm, cool head if you can. Set yourself up to understand that Marco might not have made the decisions you wanted him to make in the moment, but he made them because he cares so much about you. It makes a difference."

"Thank you," I told her. "That's great advice. I'm so glad I came over."

"Anytime," she said. "You were there for me when I needed it the most. I'm happy to return the favor. You and Marco were visiting possible locations for the Watering Can, and you dropped everything to come and help me through my crisis." She chortled. "And if you recall, the crisis was that I was making out with the man of my dreams. Literally the hottest make-out session I've ever had in my entire life. And I ran out of there like a lunatic. So that's what friends are for—we drop everything for each other."

"I'm beyond grateful that I have such a great group of dependable friends," I said. "It's saved me thousands of dollars in therapy." I still spent money on therapy, of course. But having great girlfriends certainly helped.

"Me, too," Summer said. "Now we get to talk about the fun stuff. The Watering Can logo is on its way. I think you really going to love it. I did three iterations, like usual. But I'm really excited about one of them in particular. It's a flowerpot made of flowers in bright colors, heavy on the pinks and greens. I think it fits you and the concept to a T."

"I'm so excited to see it."

The door to the loft opened, and Xander Scott strode in.

Summer sprang out of her seat before she remembered I was there.

"Hello, Eve," Xander said as he shrugged off his jacket, giving Summer a quick hug and kiss, his arm lingering around her waist. "It's nice to see you."

"What are you doing here?" Summer asked her man, patting his chest. "It's Monday at noon. I thought you had a meeting."

Xander winked. "I do. With you. I figured we'd grab a bite to eat if you were free. I wanted to surprise you."

That was my cue to make myself scarce.

I stood, walking the teacup into the kitchen, which was basically a few feet away. "You guys have a great lunch. I'll catch up with you later this week, Summer."

She moved forward, shaking her head. "No. You came over to see the logo. We had a date before Xander and I had a date. Let's do the business stuff first. He can wait."

"I can absolutely wait," Xander agreed. "I'll just grab some food and head back to the office. It's not a problem at all." This hot hunk of a guy was a tax attorney.

They were both so nice, but I shook my head adamantly. "Absolutely not. Forward me the images, and I'll take a look, then we can meet in a day or two. There is no way I'm standing in the way of your date. Besides, my brain is so full of everything we talked about, I'm not sure I can focus on what you need to show me anyway." Before Summer could argue further, I slipped by them and made my way to the door. "I'll keep you posted about Marco. Bye, Xander!" I exited quickly and efficiently.

Before the door shut completely, I heard Xander say, "Goodbye, Eve. Sorry to crash your date."

I giggled as I went down the stairs of the gorgeously refurbished mansion.

Summer was about to have an infinitely better lunch than me, and I didn't begrudge her one second of it. I'd once been a proud member of the Nooner Club, and I was certain I would be again.

I just had to get Marco to tell me what was going on.

Chapter 19

ARE YOU HOME?

My phone had beeped while I was in the bathroom getting ready for bed. It was Marco. I tapped back a reply.

YES. JUST GETTING READY FOR BED.

He responded quickly.

I KNOW IT'S LATE, BUT CAN I COME OVER?

My heart began to pound.

We'd talked during the day, after I'd been at Summer's, and he'd asked me to dinner. I'd made an excuse about being busy with some accounting work, which had been true for the most part. I'd assured him that everything was fine when he'd asked. I just hadn't been ready to have a big conversation with him yet and knew once I saw him, things would begin to tumble out.

It was pushing eleven. I'd assumed he'd gone home from work and had had an early night.

SURE. I'D LOVE TO SEE YOU.

I'M ACTUALLY CLOSE. I'LL BE THERE IN FIVE.

My eyebrows shot up.

He didn't live that far away, but getting from downtown to my neighborhood in Capitol Hill took about fifteen minutes.

OKAY. I'LL SEE YOU THEN.

I stood for a moment, wondering what was going on. Marco hadn't said anything worrisome, but there was suddenly a pit in my stomach. It was a little out of the ordinary that we hadn't seen each other over the past few nights. We'd spent a lot of time together since we'd started dating. He'd likely noticed the distance and probably wanted to talk about it.

That meant that we'd likely be getting to the bottom of things.

Like, right now.

Was I ready? It didn't really matter. It was happening.

Shrugging a robe on over my pajamas, I went into the kitchen and poured myself a glass of wine. It couldn't hurt.

My intercom buzzed a few minutes later, and I green-lit Marco up without checking to see if it was him.

A soft knocking sounded on the door a minute later.

"Hi there," I said as I opened it.

He leaned in to kiss me, which I accepted readily, then stepped back so he could come inside.

"I'm glad you're up," he said as he walked into my living room. It looked as if he was still in his work clothes—a navy button-up tucked into a pair of black slacks. He looked amazing. But it was weird he was still dressed like that. That meant he'd probably gone out.

"Did you end up going out after work?" I asked, following him into my living room.

He sat on the couch and patted the cushion next to him. "I have something to tell you, and it couldn't wait until tomorrow."

"Okay." I eased down next to him, so close our knees touched.

He ran a hand through his hair, his gaze off in the distance somewhere. I didn't want to rush him.

When he was ready, he said, "I haven't exactly been honest with you about a few things."

I held my breath, waiting for him to continue. My heart was galloping. This was it. We were in it.

"I know you've noticed I've been dodging your questions about my parents." He shook his head as it bobbed downward. "I just couldn't bring myself to talk about it until now." He gripped his hands together between his knees, his shoulders hunched forward. "When I went to tell my parents that Yasmine and I were breaking up, I didn't actually do it."

"What?" I was confused. He'd come home with a whole story. "You didn't tell them at all? *Any* of it?"

He set his head in his hands, shaking his head. "No."

A beach ball was lodged in my throat. I was having a hard time breathing. "Why?"

"When I got there, I could tell they'd been crying." He glanced up, turning his gaze to meet mine, his eyes full of emotion. My heart continued to beat recklessly. By the looks of it, this was going to be a tough story. "They were trying to hide it from me, being overly cheerful, trying to act like everything was okay. I kept asking what was wrong, but they wouldn't answer. Instead, my mom wanted to feed me, which was her usual. We sat down at the table and began to eat the meal she'd prepared, and I was about to tell them that the engagement was off, when my mom launched into how much she loved Yasmine and how happy she was for us. That went on for a while. Then, abruptly, she started to cry." He rubbed his face with his hands.

I ran my hand up and down his arm, giving him comfort. That would've been enough to crush him. He loved his mom so much. Seeing her in distress would've been hard.

He took a few moments to compose himself. We sat together in silence.

"I asked her what was wrong. And kept asking until she told me." He took a deep breath. "They found out that day that her cancer has returned, and the prognosis isn't great. But she wanted me to know that she was extremely happy to see me settled and in love and that even if she wouldn't be alive to see her grandchildren, she knew that Yasmine and I would be amazing parents. She went on and on." My heart broke for him. "I just…I just couldn't add to her stress and worry. I couldn't tell them that the engagement was off." His eyes darted to mine, holding my gaze. "But I knew it was a temporary decision. I'd fix it soon. Like in a week or two, after she wasn't in as much shock, and we had a set plan for fighting the cancer." His head bobbed downward again in defeat. "But that didn't happen. I kept putting it off. I just couldn't distress her further. I'm so sorry. I should've leveled with you from the beginning, but I didn't want to disappoint you either. Breaking the engagement was a big deal. A defining moment. It legitimized our relationship. I just thought I'd do it soon, and everything would be fine, and you didn't have to know that I chickened out."

My heart was a mushy mess. "First of all, I'm so, so sorry that the cancer has returned. That's awful news. Your family is your top priority. I completely understand why you didn't want to tell your parents in that moment. I would've supported that decision. But as time passed, why not tell me? It was so much harder to keep it from me." I continued to rub his back. "I would've been totally fine with your choice to wait—I *am* fine with it. We can go at your pace, whatever you feel comfortable with."

He lifted his head, turning toward me, a half smile on his face. "When I left to go speak with them, we were both so upbeat. It was the beginning of a brand-new chapter in our lives. You were excited, and so was I. Then, when I got back, you were so hopeful. So sincere. You asked me how it went, and I could tell it mattered a lot to you. I didn't want to ruin it and make you think you weren't the most important thing to me, because you are. I didn't want you to feel that this relationship isn't real and valid, because it is." He moved, gathering me in his arms, resting his head in the crook of my neck. "You're so incredible," he murmured. "I couldn't look you in the eye and tell you that I didn't tell my parents the engagement had been called off. It felt like a betrayal. I just figured I could handle it. That I'd tell them in a week or two, and everything would be fine."

We held each other for a long moment. I stroked the back of his head.

"I'm so sorry you had to shoulder that burden by yourself," I whispered. "We haven't known each other well that long, but just so you know in the future, family is incredibly important to me. The health and happiness of your parents and your relationship with them are all paramount in my mind. I've been completely stressing about this. If you'd told me the truth, I would've understood completely."

"I knew that in my heart." He drew back, his hands gripping my arms. "You're a very generous, loving soul. And still, I just couldn't bring myself to disappoint you. We were in this happy little bubble together, and I felt like if I told you the truth, it would burst. I know it's silly, and as time went on, and my mom started her new chemo treatments, I kept thinking I would tell them, and things would work out, but I couldn't. Then I'd see you, knowing that I didn't tell you the truth, and it killed me." He shook his head. "I just wanted everything to be perfect. Yasmine and I were in a less-than-par relationship for a long time, then suddenly I was with you. It was such a wonderful feeling. It felt too risky to deliver bad news so quickly."

Sounded just like Marco.

"That's pretty much what Yasmine thought," I confided. "She felt that whatever this was, you were just overthinking it and didn't want to hurt my feelings."

"You talked to her about me?" he asked. "I don't blame you. If something was going on with you, I probably would've reached out to one of your friends eventually."

"I did chat with her," I told him. "We went out for drinks last night. I knew you were keeping information from me about your parents. But I actually thought you'd told them everything, and they were so angry they threatened to disown you. She didn't think that was a correct assumption. She knows your parents love you beyond reason. She felt whatever it was you were keeping from me you were doing because you were worried about how I would take the news so early in our relationship."

"It didn't even occur to me that you'd think something like that, that my parents would disown me," he said. "I'm so sorry. I feel even more awful about keeping everything from you now. I have to admit I've been so distracted and worried about my mom, it's definitely clouded my judgment."

"That's understandable. Having your mom battle cancer is a big deal. I'm glad you can be so supportive to her during it. I'm actually relieved that you've been talking to them, because I thought you weren't."

How could this admission feel like a relief? Not the cancer, of course. But I was so relieved we were getting it all out on the table. My heart rate slowing back to normal.

"I've been going to her chemo appointments, which happen over lunch. I sit with her and keep her company," he said. "I knew if I told you, you'd want to send her a card, or do something else nice. But because she didn't know you existed and still thought I was engaged to Yasmine, I couldn't do it. I felt so bad about it. This entire thing snowballed beyond the scope of what I thought possible." He brought his hand up to my cheek, running his thumb along my face. "If I could take it back and do it over again, I would. I would've confided in you immediately. I can't go back, but I made it right tonight. I finally told them about us."

"You did?"

He nodded. "My mom was admitted to the hospital overnight for observation. I found out right as I was getting off of work, so I went straight over. I've been there all night, which is why I was close. I hadn't planned on telling them, because we were all freaked out she was in the hospital in the first place, but I ended up spilling everything as the night went on—about Yasmine and me breaking up, about getting involved with you, about keeping the truth from you. I told them I'm crazy happy with you. I gushed about you. I told them about the first time we met. We cried together, then we laughed, then we cried again. It was cathartic to get everything off my chest." He rested his forehead against mine. "I'm so sorry. About everything. I hope you can forgive me."

Tears streamed down both of our faces.

"I forgive you," I whispered, my hands on his cheeks. "We'd only been together three or four days when you went to tell them your engagement was over. We barely knew each other. I support you not wanting to hurt your parents. You're such a sweet, generous person. It makes total sense. I don't blame you for not wanting to tell me either. We *were* in this happy bubble together. So much so that I didn't realize things weren't adding up with your parents until almost two months later. All I could see was our happiness. Then, when I began to notice that you weren't talking about your family or telling me about going to see them, that's when I figured out something was wrong."

"I know. You began to ask about them more often," he said. "And I should've addressed it right then and there instead of trying to dodge those questions. But I kept getting more and more worried that if you knew I'd kept the truth from you, for almost two months by that point, it would somehow dampen what we'd begun to build together. But the damage came anyway. You've been pulling away from me. When you left the other night after I made the call to my cousin Sophia, I knew I had to make things right. It was even more glaring when you didn't want to go to dinner with me tonight. I was completely miserable."

"Is that why you ended up telling your parents tonight?" I asked. "While your mom was in the hospital."

"Maybe? I didn't go over there with the intent of telling them, but I knew I had to very soon. My mother was admitted because she has a weird rash brought on by the chemo. We didn't know if it was really serious or if she was having some kind of allergic reaction to a new drug. I certainly didn't think I'd tell them while she was lying in a hospital bed. But the timing felt right. She, my dad, and I were reminiscing about things as a family, trying to keep things light, telling funny stories. And it just sort of came out. I was so relieved, I just kept talking and talking."

"You said you all cried together."

"We did." He brushed his lips lightly against mine, one hand behind my neck, his fingers splayed in my hair. "They were tears of happiness. For everyone. I told them all about you, going back to college, the twenty dollars, the sweatshirt, meeting you at the bank, my feelings for you, everything that went on with Yasmine, how Yasmine reconnected with Matt. We laughed, and we cried, but it was all because we were happy. They can't wait to meet you."

I drew back from him. "Really?"

"Really." He kissed me again. "By the end, they were saying our relationship had to be fate, that we must be meant to be together. They said our story resembled how they met. My dad ended up meeting my mom a few years before they actually started dating. He'd been intimidated by her beauty and grace. His words." Marco grinned. "It was very sweet. My mom gave me an extra-long hug before I left, telling me to go find you immediately to tell you the truth and assuring me that you would understand because my heart was in the right place and your heart was open. Then she reminded me to let you know that they're excited to meet someone who makes me so incredibly happy." A tear rolled down his cheek. "It made me feel wonderful and sad at the same time. Wonderful that they're so ready to embrace you, and sad because I obviously made the wrong choice by keeping things from everyone."

"I don't think you made the wrong choice," I whispered, my voice catching. I was having a hard time getting the words out. "If you'd told them that night, when they'd just found out about the cancer returning, things could've gone differently. You could've easily given them a bigger burden to bear in the moment." I cleared my throat. "But you listened to your heart, and I can't argue with that. Next time, you'll just have to tell me sooner."

"There won't be a next time." He leaned in for a kiss. It was sweet and soulful. All of our combined emotions were wrapped up in it. "I know you can handle anything. You're my absolute rock. Not telling you the truth has been weighing on me so heavily, I can assure you it's not going to happen again. We are in this together, through thick and thin."

"Yes, we are." I stood, grabbing his hand.

As we walked toward my bedroom, I knew I'd never been happier.

CHAPTER 20

A re you nervous?" Poppy asked me for the fourth time.

We stood in front of the newly installed coolers at the Watering Can. I opened one of the doors and grabbed a bucket of fresh tulips, then added in a few hydrangeas, three buttercups, and some myrtle for greenery.

I'd ordered a few dozen of each flower from a local wholesaler to assess the quality, and I was impressed. This company was definitely going on our list. I planned to order as much local product as I could.

I brought the flowers to the tall table we'd stationed in the middle of the room and grabbed two vases. "Of course I'm nervous. I'm meeting Marco's parents for the first time. What do you think? Lavender or salmon? The flowers are all in peach and yellow tones, so salmon is the logical choice, but lavender poses a nice contrast."

Poppy bit her lip, then gestured at the salmon. "I'm a fan of monochromatic things. I think it'll be a smash."

I hoped so.

It'd been a few weeks since Marco had told his parents about me. His mom had been released from the hospital a week and a half ago. She'd ended up being under observation for three days, and the situation had been a little more critical than they'd first thought. I hadn't felt right about meeting his mom and dad during such a trying time.

She was doing much better now.

In fact, her last PET scan had shown that the tumors were shrinking again, like they had the first time around. Everyone was cautiously optimistic.

"Yoo-hoo!" Yasmine called as she came through the back door. "Where are you?"

"We're in here," I called from the refrigeration room.

"Man, it looks fabulous in here," Yasmine said. "It's been a while since I stopped by." She walked to the front of the shop. "Nice. It's all coming together. I love all these pots and vases. Can't wait until they're up for sale. I'm buying a ton." She made her way into the room we were in. "Hey, Poppy." She gave us each a quick hug.

"Hey, yourself," Poppy said. "Looking glamorous, as usual. It's not fair that you're always putting us to shame. I actually thought I killed it today. But compared to you, I look like Drizella playing dress-up as the real princess goes to the ball."

Yasmine flipped her hair over her shoulder and giggled. "Thanks. I tried. And what are you talking about? You look great. Those capris are totally on point. I need a pair." She came up to the table. "What's going on here?"

"These are for Aleah." I nodded at the blooms I was arranging in the vase. "I hope she likes them."

"She's going to absolutely gobble them up." Yasmine took a seat on one of the stools. "I have it on good authority she loves flowers. She's so excited that you and Marco are running the shop together. I was finally able to speak with her a few days ago, and she was super upbeat. Literally brimming with joy. It was so good to hear. That woman deserves to live a nice long life. She's the absolute best."

"Her tumors are shrinking," I said. "Everyone's very excited."

"She told me," Yasmine replied. "But that's not the first thing she wanted to talk about. Before anything else, she made me tell her all about Matt. When I was done, she said my joy was contagious. It was odd, yet wonderful to hear. This was someone who I thought for a long time was going to be my mother-in-law. I'm so glad she's accepted everything and still wants to talk to me. It means so much. It's really put my heart at ease." She put a hand over her heart. "In fact, my parents have taken notice of how the Cruzes have received the news of our breakup and have readjusted accordingly. It's been so much better all around. I'm ecstatic."

"That's great," I told her. "I'm so glad Marco ended up telling his parents you guys broke up before your mother got a hold of Aleah. That would've been awkward. She would've been the one to tell them about the engagement ending."

"For sure," Yasmine agreed. "But the thought that Marco hadn't told his parents wasn't in any of our brains." She tapped the side of her head with a beautifully done deep-purple nail. "I would've thought a lot of things, but not that. Not only did he tell you a false story, I got the same one, too. I never questioned it."

"But after we heard everything about his mother's cancer," Poppy said, "it made total sense. I mean, he couldn't crush her with that kind of news when she was in the middle of getting that other kind of awful news."

"Yes," Yasmine said. "I'm glad he waited. It would've been a lot for them to take in. But not telling us." She moved her hand between her and me. "That was out of character. But I understand why he did it." She grinned at me, bouncing in her seat. "Do you want to know why? Do you?"

I laughed. "I'm not sure if I do. But tell me anyway, because I know it's about to come tumbling out. It looks like you're about to pop."

"It's because he's in L-O-V-E." She took her time spelling out the word with lots of gushy exaggeration.

"You know not of what you speak," I told her.

"She knows exactly of what she speaks," Poppy chirped, nodding along. "And he totally is. I mean, the man flew down to Montecito at the last minute to get you out of jail before you were even dating. You guys drove back together and basically settled the whole deal. He's been head over heels since the very beginning."

"He has not," I protested. "We haven't said that word to each other. We've literally only been dating for a little over two months. It's way too early."

"Yeah, but you've been in love with him for eight years," Yasmine pointed out. "Don't lie to us, because we know."

"Yeah, we're the great and powerful Oz." Poppy wiggled her fingers like she was casting a spell. "Nothing gets past us. The man was insanely desperate to make sure nothing rocked the boat. The boat of *love*, that is. Or maybe we should call it the

Love Boat?"

Yasmine leaned forward, waggling both eyebrows. "Speaking of boats, you went for a ride on one and were pretty scarce on the details. Why is that? Because it was full of *love.*" She winked, giggling.

I chortled. These two were clearly on a roll. "It's true I've lusted after him for eight years, but we're not at the L-O-V-E stage. I haven't even met his parents." I nodded toward the vase because my hands were full of flowers. "Case in point. I'm putting this beautiful arrangement together to make sure I give the best first impression possible."

"They're going to adore you," Yasmine cooed. "Flowers or not. They're going to see how sweet, smart, and nice you are and fall madly in love on the spot, just like their son. It's going to be a slam dunk."

"I love slam dunks!" Poppy squealed. "Can either of you sprinkle some slam-dunk powder on me? Please?" She held her arms out. "Tell me that exists. In fact, I'll take some right over and dump it in Leo's latte. Yes, the man likes a mocha swirl latte with oat milk. No judgment."

Both Yasmine and I giggled.

"No judgment here," I said. "But I'm pretty sure slam-dunk powder does not exist."

"Maybe I should just hire a witch?" Poppy contemplated that, sitting on the stool next Yasmine. "There's a new crystal shop down the street. They employ Wiccans, right? They must have some sort of love potion. Or have a mortar and pestle that can crunch up some crystals. Crystals provide good chi, then love naturally flows, right?"

"I don't think that's how chi works." I chuckled.

"I take it things are still not great with Leo?" Yasmine said. "That man doesn't need any love potion. He needs to be sat down and told he's about to lose a hell of a woman if he doesn't get his act together."

"His act is in disrepair," Poppy replied glumly. "I'm like a broken record with this, but it bums me out. Not ready to give up, yet. But getting close. Very, very close."

"How about going on a double date with me and Matt?" Yasmine asked. "He's coming in next week." She could not mask her excitement. "He's only here for the weekend, but I think this is going to be the big decider. We're going to choose if we want to be in a committed relationship or not. Once we do, all bets are off. We'd love to have dinner with you and Leo while he's here, though. That would be so fun."

"Oh my goodness!" Poppy clapped. "That's great news and such a generous offer. But I wouldn't even know how to ask Leo to come out with us. It would be awkward. We were supposed to meet yesterday, and he didn't show. I got an apology text from him later, saying he was taking care of some business. No further explanation."

"That's hard," Yasmine commented. "What if Matt and I simply stop by the bar while you guys are working? Then we just casually roll it into all of us going to get something to eat together. That could work."

"That sounds like a great idea," I encouraged.

"Yeah, maybe," Poppy said. "Let me think about it."

"Just text me," Yasmine said. "I'm happy to help."

"I appreciate that," Poppy said. "I'm such the downer these days. I apologize to you both. I feel like I have my hat constantly out to accept tokens of kindness. What I should actually do is move on with my life. But, then again, he's still giving me mixed signals. When he is focused on me, life is very good. He dotes on me, he teases me, he looks at me like he wants to eat me for breakfast. My tummy gets all fluttery, my heart races, my pits sweat. It's wonderful. Then, the next day, it's like a cyborg clone is at the brewpub instead." She shook her head. "He's distant, unexpressive, distracted by his phone. He's just a whole 'nother guy. I have no idea what to think."

"It sounds like he might be dealing with something stressful," Yasmine said. "Maybe a relative is sick, or something's happened he's not ready to share yet."

"That could very well be," Poppy replied. "But I don't think so. I've asked enough probing questions. He dodges most of them, but if it was a family member, I think he would say something. I'm pretty sure it's his ex, Pamela. I just have this feeling. She broke his heart once already, and if he picks her again, everything we've been working toward is over. All the flirting, all the closeness, all the time spent together will have been for nothing."

"It hasn't been for nothing," I assured her. "You've been building up a nice foundation, becoming friends first. He's not picking his ex over you. He might be dealing with some things now, but he'll come around."

"I've only met the guy a few times, when I've stopped by the pub," Yasmine said. "But he doesn't strike me as a guy who would lead you on for no reason. He seems well aware of himself and wouldn't want to be in a toxic relationship again. Pamela might be trying to seek his attention, and he's dealing with it. It makes sense that he wouldn't want to tell you that his ex is giving him a hard time. Because you're not in a relationship, you're going to have to be patient until he works it out and is ready to share the details."

"You're right," Poppy lamented. "I just wish he felt like he could share this with me. I'd totally be supportive."

"As we know from experience," I said, "men tend to keep emotional issues close to the vest. Not all of them. That'd be a gross generalization. But it happened to me, and it happened to Summer. Xander didn't readily share everything that was going on with him. Marco was too concerned about hurting my feelings to tell the truth. Leo's probably worried that you'll opt out if you know what's happening with him behind the scenes. He doesn't want to start something with you until the other stuff is finished."

"Why can't they be more like us?" Poppy made a pouty face and crossed her arms. "We talk excessively about our issues. When something's wrong, we spew word diarrhea everywhere." She splayed her hands across the table. "It's an emotional mess, but such a relief at the same time. It's so cathartic to get it all out there, we do it again and again."

I giggled. "He's going to come around. I know he will." I threaded the last myrtle stem into the vase. It looked phenomenal. A few peach-colored roses, and it would be complete. I walked to a cooler and pulled open the door, grabbing three roses. Then I took my shears to the thorns and placed the stems in the vase. "How does it look?"

"Like pure joy," Poppy said. "For real. Gorgeous."

"It looks like it was assembled with love," Yasmine said. "Just plain old caring, empathetic love. Not the L-O-V-E kind. I honestly can't wait for you to meet Marco's parents. We're going to have to go out for coffee in the morning, because I'll want to hear all about it."

"Let's do breakfast." Poppy clapped. "Summer can probably make it, and Jenny might be free. She's working a more normal schedule these days, something like eleven to eleven. Dang, they make those doctors-in-training work hard."

"Breakfast it is," I told them. "I'll text the group chat tonight with a few highlights." I set the entire vase on a shelf in a cooler. I was meeting Marco in a couple hours. Then we were picking up food and heading over to his parents. They lived in a suburb about twenty-five minutes away. I had a ton of nervous energy, but I was extremely excited.

"Don't be overwhelmed when Aleah breaks out the photo albums," Yasmine cautioned. "She loves to reminisce, and the pictures of Marco as a child are utterly precious. She has a stack of them this high." She made a wide gap between her hands. "No, probably this high." She spread her hands farther apart. "I'm not joking."

"I can't wait to see them," I said. "I love that kind of stuff. Marco had to have been an adorable child."

"Oh, he was. Believe me. He particularly loves the potty-training pictures." Yasmine giggled. "He'll make a big fuss about them, but he secretly loves it."

"What are you going to wear?" Poppy asked. "I'm assuming not the yoga pants and plaid shirt you have on right now."

I glanced down the front of my outfit. "No, definitely not this. I brought my light green sundress. Let me grab it." I went to the utility closet, which had a fair amount of space inside, to get it. As I pulled open the door, memories of Marco bringing me in here a few short months ago, kissing me for the first time, popped into my mind with bright clarity. What an avalanche of events that had created. I pulled my dress from the hanger, smiling, remembering his firm lips and the crazy need I'd felt while kissing him. Back in the refrigeration room, I held the dress up to my chest and swung my hips around. "Is this too summery?"

"No, it's perfect," Poppy said.

"Completely adorable," Yasmine said. "You look like a beautiful flower with your gorgeous red hair and green body. A beautiful red rose. It's totally fitting."

"You guys are too good to me," I said.

"We're the truth squad, dropping truth bombs left and right." Poppy snorted. "You have this all sewn up. It's going to be fabulous, and they're going to love you."

"I hope so."

We were about to see.

CHAPTER 21

Marco grabbed my hand and gave it a reassuring squeeze. "Are you ready? Feeling okay?" We'd just pulled up at his parents' house, a lovely one-and-a-half story stucco home in a suburb full of tree-lined streets.

I brought my hands up to my hair to make sure it was all in place, flipping down the visor to look in the mirror while rubbing my lips together. "I'm nervous, but excited."

"My mom texted me no less than ten times today. She's brimming with excitement. She didn't know what to do with herself, since we're bringing dinner, so she insisted on making homemade baklava for dessert, even though she's supposed to be resting. Hers is the best I've ever had. The pastry is light and flaky, and she brushes it with this amazing honey-lemon glaze." He chuckled. "I wouldn't be surprised if she's made a bunch of desserts for us to sample. Her favorite thing in the world is to cook."

"I can't wait to taste it all," I told him, leaning down to retrieve the flowers that I'd braced between my feet on the way over. "It's so sweet of her to cook for us."

"It's one of her top favorite things to do. There will be a lot of Moroccan and Spanish meals in our future, sometimes a fusion of both. She's an amazing cook. Every meal is made with love." He opened his car door and stepped out, opening up the side door to take out the food.

We'd ended up ordering Indian from one of our favorite places.

I got out, managing to hold the flowers with one hand. Marco flashed me a smile as we made our way up the walk.

Before we could reach the front door, it whipped open. Marco's father, Antonio, stood there. He was shorter than Marco and a bit stocky, his formerly dark hair heavily streaked with gray above his ears. He waved in greeting as he propped open the screen. "There you two are," he called jovially. "We thought you'd never arrive." He gave his stomach an exaggerated rub. "We're dying of hunger over here."

Marco laughed. "I happen to know how many casseroles are in the freezer and refrigerator at this very moment. There's no way you're starving."

"Get in here and give your father a hug." Antonio coaxed Marco forward and embraced him, slapping a hand on his back. "It's good to see you, son." He stepped to the side. "Now please introduce me to your new, special friend."

"Antonio Cruz, this is Evangeline Foster, Eve for short. Eve, this is my father, Antonio."

I started to move forward, unsure what to do, but Antonio took a step outside and enveloped me in a bear hug. "Nice to meet you, Eve. So happy to welcome you into our home."

"Hey," a voice called from inside the house. "No fair leaving me out of the introductions! Come inside."

Antonio chortled. "We are on our way in, dear." He guided me through the door Marco was holding open, his arm loosely around my shoulders. Once inside, we turned to the left into a cozy living room filled with knickknacks, family photos, and comfortable throws. Aleah was sitting on the couch, a blanket draped over her legs.

"Come." She beckoned. "No need to be shy. They're making me rest on the couch like an invalid, or I would've greeted you at the door." She had a beautiful multicolored scarf wrapped around her head.

Marco had told me that the new rounds of chemo had made her hair fall out quickly this time. She was doing better with it the second time around, but she was still sad she was losing her hair.

I walked toward her, holding the vase in front of me. I couldn't exactly plop it in her lap. I hoped I wasn't messing this up. "These are for you," I managed.

"They are utterly beautiful," she crooned, taking the vase with one hand and waving me forward with the other. I bent over to give her a one-armed hug. As I stood back up, she brought the flowers to her nose and scented each one of them. "This is the best-smelling arrangement I've ever received. Thank you for thinking of me." She nodded toward her husband. "Antonio, please take these and put them on the table as the centerpiece. That way, we can enjoy them for the entire evening."

Antonio came and got the vase, sniffing the flowers as he walked into the adjoining dining room. "These are beautiful. So robust. Your shop is going to be a thrilling success if this is what you're going to offer. I see nothing but dollar signs."

Marco chuckled. "I hope so. Dollar signs are what we're after. Hello, Mom." He gave his mother a hug and a kiss on the cheek. She held on for a long moment. "You're looking well today."

"I've been feeling much better these past few days," she said. "It's such a relief after all of the side effects." She directed her gaze at me. "I'm sure my son has filled you in, but they tried a new drug that hasn't exactly agreed with me, although it seems to be fighting the cancer very well. So I will soldier through."

"I'm so glad you're feeling better," I told her. "Marco has been very concerned."

She patted the cushion next to her. "Come and sit with me. Enough talk about sickness. I want to hear all about you. Every single detail."

"Maybe we can save some of the questions until later. Maybe after dinner," Marco suggested lightly, grinning at me. He'd prepared me for this, saying his mother would ask all about my life, my hobbies, my family, everything.

"Nonsense," his mother said. "Eve is going to join me here, and you and your father are going to go out and fix the garage door. Here, hand me those photo albums." She beckoned toward a nearby table. "Eve is going to want to see you as a child. I have so many stories to tell."

I sat next to her. "It's totally fine," I told Marco. "Go out with your dad and fix the garage. We can eat after."

"Perfect," Antonio said, coming back into the room. "I put the food in the oven to warm. It will keep."

"You said you were dying of starvation," Marco joked, "but suddenly we have time to fix the garage door that's been broken for no less than three years."

"I just tracked down the part I needed," Antonio said. "It finally came into the machine shop over on Fourth Street. Stop wasting time, and let's get this done. We have to keep your mother happy." He chuckled as he turned and headed back into the kitchen.

Marco lifted the albums that were sitting on the table and set them on his mother's lap. Then he leaned over and kissed me on the forehead. "We'll be back in shortly." He turned to his mom. "Try not to talk her ear off too much, and keep those potty-training pictures to yourself."

"Shush, you," Aleah said. "We're starting with your baby pictures and going from there." She stated it matter-of-factly. "Potty training is nothing to be ashamed about. Every child goes through it. You will do it with your own children. And we will laugh about the pictures later."

"Mom," Marco complained. "You can at least wait until the second visit to show Eve pictures of me sitting naked on a toilet."

"Fine, I will acquiesce to your wishes," his mother said. "Now, shoo." She flicked her wrist. "Go help your father." Once he left the room, Aleah turned to me, grinning. "Let's start with the potty training, shall we?"

I giggled. "Whatever you're willing to show me, I'd love to see. My parents have very few baby pictures of me and my brother. I can't wait to see all the adorable pictures of Marco."

"Why do you have so few photos?" she asked.

I hadn't planned to get into that with her, but if we were going to have real conversations, it was going to come up eventually. "My parents went through a pretty bitter divorce starting when

I was two and my brother was a newborn. There wasn't a lot of time or wonderful family moments to stop and take pictures. Or so I've been told. Don't get me wrong, we do have a few. There are the standard ones at holidays and birthdays, but very few day-to-day, around-the-house ones. I don't think it would've even occurred to my mother to take a potty-training picture. Then, when my parents finalized the divorce a few years later, I went to live with my mom, and my brother went to live with my dad. Both my parents worked full-time, so they were gone a lot." I shrugged. "It wasn't as bad as it sounds, because I didn't know anything different. I was happy for the most part. My mom and I have a great relationship. But as we got older, my brother came over less and less, and I went to my father's less and less. It was just easier that way."

Aleah made a clucking noise as she patted the top of my hand. "It sounds like your parents made the best decisions they could during a very tough time. Not every parent gets it right, but most of them do try. There aren't any rulebooks out there to follow. At least I haven't found any perfect ones. I would love to see the baby photos you do have one day. I'm sure you're as adorable as my Marco, with all that red hair and your gorgeous smile." She patted my hand a few more times, then opened the first book, pointing to a picture of a newborn Marco swaddled in a hospital blanket with little ducks all over it.

My heart literally melted.

This woman was truly a gift. Yasmine hadn't been lying in the least. She was so comfortable and easy, full of love. "He's so cute. Look at all that hair."

"Oh yes, he was born with a full head of dark hair. Wait till you see him when he begins to crawl."

We'd been at the albums for a while when Marco and his father finally came back in. We'd been laughing and cooing over Marco. The potty-training pics had been hilarious. He'd been so proud of himself for getting it right.

"It's time to eat," Marco said, taking my hand and helping me off the couch, then his mother. As we walked into the dining room, where Antonio was busy placing the food on the table, Marco leaned over and whispered in my ear, "How's it going?"

"It couldn't be better," I assured him. "Everything is perfect. Your parents are amazing."

"Oh my goodness, Marco's mom sounds precious," Jenny said, taking a fork to her pancakes. "And so kind. If you and Marco get married, an amazing mother-in-law is a rarity that needs to be cherished. Not saying that mine isn't great, because she is. But she has her moments. Getting the gold standard in-laws is hard to come by."

Summer set her orange juice on the table. It was nine thirty in the morning, and we were gathered at the Egg's Nest for breakfast and a debriefing. "I haven't met Xander's mom yet, but we've video-chatted a few times, and she's completely lovely. But Aleah really does sound like the gold standard. You're so lucky."

I finished a bite of omelet and reached for my coffee. "She was beyond amazing, and so was Antonio. We had such a lovely dinner. I can't wait to go back. And honestly, the baklava she made was out of this world. She promised to teach me how to make it the next time we come over."

"Her cooking is to die for. So yummy," Yasmine said. "And

Matt's mom is standard nice. She tries, but it's not as effortless as it is with Aleah. I'm going to miss seeing her on a weekly basis."

"Speaking of that," I told Yasmine. "She wants you and Matt to join us for dinner sometime soon. She'll be sad if you don't keep in touch. She asked all about you and would absolutely welcome regular visits from you."

"See?" Yasmine shook her head. "How many women would be that gracious after you and her only son break up? I didn't expect them to be so nice about it. I mean, I knew they would be okay eventually, but I expected them to have hurt feelings. Kind of makes me wish we'd done it sooner, but we were so scared to let everybody down. Hindsight is everything. I'm happy with how things have turned out, though. I feel very lucky."

"Marco feels the same," I said. "He's beyond relieved that his parents are fine with the news and even seem excited about the future."

"Speaking of the future, does everyone have the thirtieth marked on their calendar?" Poppy asked. "Zoe's Lager is making its debut to the world. It's less than a month away, so it'll be here before we know it."

"It's so exciting," Summer said. "And the brewpub looks beyond excellent. Poppy has done such an amazing job."

Poppy raised her finger and wagged it. "Ah, ah, ah. There's going to be no more peeking. From this day forward, everybody has to wait for the big reveal. I want it to be a surprise. I mean it."

Summer shook her head. "Um, that's not going to work for me. Xander is there so often, that means I am, too, but I promise I'll only squint sideways while I'm there."

"Obviously not you. You can't stay away from Mr. Raw Sexy for five minutes." Poppy snorted. "But everybody else has to steer clear." Crossed her arms, making it known she was serious. "Stay away or the unveiling won't be as much fun."

"Summer told me that the bar is already getting reporters and critics reaching out," Jenny said to Poppy. "I hope that's spilling over to you. A decent amount of the credit should go to you."

"A few people have reached out," Poppy replied. "Mostly in the interior design world. But it's pretty standard to have reporters and critics interested in the grand opening of a bar slash restaurant."

"She's going to get a lot of work from this," Summer asserted. "I've seen the work drawings, and they're incredible. If you manage to pull all that off, you're going to be the talk of the town."

"Maybe your old firm will want to hire you back," I suggested.

Poppy made a face as she reached for her latte. "They can try. I'm having so much fun with this job, I've decided I'm going to incorporate and everything. Interior design will be my full-time job from now on. But only on my terms, never again with a big firm."

We all hooted and hollered, and there was a round of congratulations at the table.

I raised my coffee cup. "Here's to the future and everything that comes with it."

We all clinked glasses.

I was incredibly lucky to have such great friends.

Chapter 22

Good morning," I murmured to Marco as I blinked awake. "How'd you sleep?"

Marco was reading on his phone. He smiled, leaning over to give me a kiss. "Best sleep I've had in years."

I stretched. "Me, too."

"I sleep more soundly now than I did when I was a kid."

"I bet you didn't snore as much back then." I giggled as I slid out of bed and made my way to the bathroom.

"I'm not the only one," Marco called. "But your snore is cute."

"How would you know?" I peeked around the corner. "You were sound asleep, remember?" I adored our banter.

We'd been spending most of our time together for the last few weeks, including all of our nights. Things were amazing between us.

Once I was finished in the bathroom, I threw on my robe, which had been hanging on the back of his door. I found Marco in the kitchen, making eggs. I went to the refrigerator and got out the pineapple we'd cut up yesterday.

"What's on your agenda today?" Marco asked.

"It's Yasmine's birthday. We're all meeting tonight at Giovanni's to celebrate. Matt's moving up here at the end of the month. She's over the moon. As far as my workday, I think I'll stop by the shop before I head home to catch up on some of the accounting work I've put off. We should be fully on track to open as planned. I can't believe it's almost here. It's so exciting." We'd been working hard to make our deadline, and everything was coming together perfectly. We'd secured deals with three wholesale flower companies that would deliver fresh flowers to the shop daily. We had customers coming to knock on the door, hoping we were already open. We'd ended up putting a big sign in the window, inviting everybody to our grand opening, scheduled to happen in six weeks.

He mixed the eggs around in the pan. "I'll head over to the shop with you, then drop you off at home before I head to work."

"That'll make you late to your day job." I glanced at the clock. "It's already eight thirty." Most mornings, Marco insisted on driving me home. It was sweet.

"It's fine. I have a late dinner meeting with a client, so I don't have to be at work until ten."

I came up behind him and wrapped my arms around his waist, laying my cheek against his back. He took the eggs off the stove and set down the spatula. Slowly, he turned and lifted me onto the counter, parting my robe and grinning. "Let's use this extra time wisely, shall we?"

"Mmmm, that sounds like a really great plan." My head lolled back as he tongued a nipple. The granite was cool against my thighs. Marco parted them, stroking me in languid circles as he dropped his plaid pajama pants to the floor.

I was panting in three seconds flat.

He entered me swiftly, at my urging, his pace ramping up to jackhammer immediately, just the way I liked it. He looped his arms underneath my knees, pulling me closer. I leaned back, my hands knocking into the plates.

Neither of us noticed.

I'd started an intrauterine contraceptive last week, which had been uncomfortable at first, but was glorious now.

We were making up for lost time.

Marco, true to his words, had learned all my pleasure points like he'd been competing in the Sex Olympics.

My fingers raked through his hair, urging him on He adjusted my body, scooting me forward slightly, angling me back with gentle pressure, hitting me in the absolute perfect spot.

I called out, my grip on him intensifying, holding on for dear life. I began to rock my hips, a signal that I was getting close. He groaned.

"Almost," I moaned. "Yes… Right—"

We came together. He locked himself deep inside, allowing me to enjoy the pressure as I spasmed against his rock-hard body.

Sex with him was so satisfying.

My entire body glistened with sweat.

I'd never known sex could be this good with someone else. Everything had come together for us—love, lust, sexiness, friendship, and passion. The way Marco looked at me during our interludes was nothing short of smoldering. His intensity lit me on fire like no one else ever had. The quality and quantity of my orgasms were charting new territory, and it was delectable.

He scooped me off the counter. I wrapped my legs around his waist, my arms linked around his neck as he walked us straight into the bathroom. "Your delicious eggs are going to be cold by the time we get back out there," I warned.

"I'll make more." He set me in the shower, giving me a sweet kiss as he turned on the water. This man was beyond thoughtful. He was my dream. I felt safe and amazing with him.

Life didn't get much better than this.

At least not for me.

"Then Marco said…"

"Nope. No, no, no," Poppy ordered, waving her hands. "I will hear no more. Get the 'Marco is a godlike creature who pleasures me to no end and who can do no wrong' expression off your face. We will be having none of that here tonight." She slashed her hand through the air. "You've reached your quota for the month already."

I laughed. "He *is* a godlike creature who pleasures me to no end and can do no wrong. What can I say? The man is a walking miracle." I winked.

Poppy mock-rolled her eyes, then giggled. "Okay, it's noted. Marco and his magic penis are magical. How's his mom doing?"

"Really well," I said. "The new drug is really helping. We went shopping together last weekend, and she barely needed to take a break. Last round of chemo is this week. She's making her famous tagine tonight. I'm actually thinking of selling her individually wrapped baklava at the shop. I'm looking into a food license and what it would take. We wouldn't have it all the time, but when she's up for making a few batches, it would be such a treat for the customers and a nice bit of money in her pocket. It is honestly the best food I've ever had. Like, ever."

"That's what you keep saying," Poppy groused. "But then you never have any when I come over."

I laughed. "She always sends us home with some, but it's too good not to eat with my coffee in the morning. I promise I'll save you some next time."

"You better," she said. "I'm so excited that everything is going well with them."

"Me, too," I said. "And get this, once Matt moves here, the four of us are going over for dinner once a month. They're really excited to meet Matt, and I know they miss Yasmine, even if they don't tell me directly. She's like a daughter to them, and I want to make sure she feels welcome in their lives, especially since her parents are so far away."

"This is definitely a fairy-tale ending for all of you," Poppy commented. "And you guys deserve it."

Summer and Jenny came through the door of Giovanni's together, both carrying gifts for Yasmine. We waved. Once they were seated, Summer asked, "Where's the birthday girl?"

"And what's the big surprise?" Jenny asked. "I'm literally dying. Matt sounds like such an incredible sweetheart. I can't wait to meet him. Yasmine's going to be floored when she finds out he set something special up for her."

"First of all," Poppy started, "Annabel can't make it. She's out with Stephanie. Some work thing Stephanie asked her to go to. It's the first time my sister is meeting Stephanie's work friends. She's nervous, but excited."

Annabel's relationship was progressing quickly. Poppy had met Stephanie, but we hadn't yet. We were planning on seeing them this weekend. I was looking forward to it. Poppy had raved about her for thirty minutes straight last week, going on and on about her incredibly beautiful eyes. Poppy had a thing about looking into someone's soul through their eyes, and she adored what she'd seen in Stephanie's.

"Second, the gift isn't something physical," Poppy continued. "It's an experience. Once we're finished with dinner here, we're relocating to the Manning Theater."

"The small place where we used to see cheap movies when we were in college?" I asked.

"Yep, the very place. Apparently, Matt put together a video clip of their memories way back when, and we're all going to go watch it. He has a friend who's a tech genius, and that theater lets you rent space for cheap. Who knew?"

Jenny clapped a hand over her heart. "Oh, that sounds ridiculously sweet!"

Poppy nodded. "So yummy. She's going to be totally surprised. She's told me that Matt's not overly sentimental, but this is crazy sentimental if you ask me." Poppy leaned forward, addressing Summer and Jenny. "And you're not going to believe what this guy looks like. I know we've tried to describe him"— she motioned between the two of us—"but young Jack Reacher is a *hunk* of a man."

"Ooh, I'm up for seeing hunky men on the big screen," Jenny said. "Even if they're in a committed relationship and I prefer a man with glasses and a scalpel. Mixing it up never hurts."

The server brought over a pitcher of beer and some glasses.

Jenny got busy pouring.

"When Yasmine comes in," Poppy said, "we break out into song. Agreed?"

We all nodded as we took sips of our drinks.

"Hey." I elbowed Poppy while nodding toward the kitchen, which was open. We could see the people making food. "Isn't that Rafael? He keeps looking over here. He's practically salivating over you, and he's kind of cute. Cuter than I remember." He resembled Zac Efron a little if I squinted, though more Italian and with slicked-back hair.

"Yeah, Italian Fabio has always had a thing for you," Jenny told Poppy, glancing over her shoulder to take a look.

"Maybe he'll bring you some coupons." Summer chuckled.

"At this point, I'd have a better shot with Rafael than Leo," Poppy said.

Everyone made the appropriate *aww* sounds.

"I thought things were going better last week," I said.

"They were," she replied, taking a swig of her beer. "He seemed to have gotten out of his funk, and we were back to flirting and having a good time. At one point, we were close to kissing, but then he went right back into his funk. I have no idea what's going on, but whatever it is, it's holding his attention more than I am." Her gaze slid across the room. "Maybe I *should* go on a date with Rafael." She bit her lip. "At least then I could get some much-needed between-the-sheets time. Watching you guys all pair up has been fun, but I'm ready for my own sexual reawakening. I want to ride those multiorgasm waves everyone keeps raving about. Sounds like a blast. I'm looking to have my world *rocked*." She pounded a fist on the table.

I giggled. "I mean, it's not a terrible plan. But I wouldn't give up on Leo just yet. The way he looks at you is so intense. We just have to find out what's going on with him personally."

Summer rested her hand on Poppy's forearm. "I'm working on getting to the bottom of it, I promise. Leo hasn't shared much with Xander, but Xander keeps asking."

"I appreciate that," Poppy said. "I know there's chemistry between us. But, honestly, tonight is all about Yasmine, and we're going to keep it that way. We have plenty of time to talk about Leo and my lack of penis-driven orgasms."

We all laughed and clinked glasses.

"There she is," I said excitedly as Yasmine walked through the door, looking completely gorgeous.

Poppy began to sing "Happy Birthday," and we all joined in.

It was going to be a fun night.

EPILOGUE

Are you excited about the big reveal?" Marco asked as he took my hand. We'd parked two blocks away from the pub, because the closer spots had already been taken. It was going to be a huge crowd.

"Yes. I can't wait," I replied. "I'm sure Zoe's Lager is going to be our new favorite hangout."

"Has Poppy shared anything with you lately? Do you know what we're about to walk into?"

"No. She's been completely cagey about everything, which is directly contrary to everything about her. I actually haven't talked to her in at least a week. That's never happened in the history of our friendship."

"She's got a lot going on. I'm sure after tonight, things will calm way down for her."

"I hope so."

We arrived at the front doors. The pub was crowded, just

as predicted. Xander, Leo, and Chris had decided to make the unveiling of Zoe's Lager a grand opening instead of a soft opening with family and friends, which was understandable.

A few critics had already given the brewpub glowing reviews. It was going to be amazing.

Marco pulled the door open and ushered me inside, his hand lingering on the small of my back.

The first person we saw was Summer.

She rushed over to give me a hug. "Isn't it incredible?"

"It really is." I scanned the interior, taking it all in. Poppy had made us swear not to come over and try to sneak a peek. "I'm in awe. It's classy and comfortable, modern and chic. It's absolute perfection."

The pub had a very eclectic vibe. One wall was covered in large retro-styled pink Zs outlined in silver. The other walls were matte black. The contrast was stunning.

The lighting was excellent—not too bright, not too dim. All the fixtures looked to be made of reclaimed metal. The bar was impressive and took up the entire middle of the room. It was covered in a porous black soapstone. It was amazing. The bottom was alternating sections of corrugated metal and reclaimed wood. Booths ran on either side, every other one decorated in either a dark green or purple velvet. The floor was a wide-board reclaimed wood stained a chocolate color.

It was a visual feast.

Poppy had outdone herself. Truly. It was a masterpiece.

I was certain it would be written up in all the style columns, not only in Seattle, but across the country. If she didn't get a million jobs from this, I'd eat my shoe.

"Come on." Summer gestured. "Everybody's over here."

Marco and I followed her through the crowd to a large space behind the bar. The mood was electric, everybody laughing and enjoying themselves. One giant, long table had been set up. It looked like a few had been pushed together.

"Welcome," Xander said, reaching out to shake Marco's hand and give me a hug. "A selection of beer is on the table. They're all labeled. Try a few and let me know what you think. We're going to be changing at least three a month. We'll keep the favorites in constant rotation." He was beaming. Zoe's Lager was his dream come true. I was so happy for him.

"We will," I assured him. He and Marco began to chat, and I looked around for Poppy.

Seeing Jenny instead, I made my way over.

"Isn't this glorious?" Jenny said. "Dan and I have been racking our brains to think of a bar with decor we like better, and we can't."

"There really isn't one out there," Daniel replied. "This feels upscale, yet totally comfortable. It's very unique."

"I agree," I said. "Have you seen Poppy? She's outdone herself, and we have to give her the rave reviews she deserves."

Jenny shook her head. "I haven't heard from her in at least a week, which is totally bizarre. I'm the most out of the loop, and she always makes a supreme effort to keep me apprised of what's going on. But it's been crickets lately."

Annabel came up with her partner, Stephanie. We'd been out with them a few times. They were adorable and completely in love. Stephanie was taller than Annabel, which aided her in her career as a semipro volleyball player. She had long blonde hair, a smattering of freckles, and legs for days. They were a stunning pair.

"Have you seen my sister?" Annabel glanced around. "This is supposed to be her shining moment. Where the hell is she? You'd think she'd be crooning about what an awesome job she's done."

I shook my head. "Jenny and I were just discussing that. She's made herself pretty scarce lately."

"Yeah, I've been spending a lot of time at Steph's, but when I was over grabbing stuff yesterday, she was running around, mumbling about drastic measures and old flames. Nothing really coherent, which is not completely uncommon. She brushed me off when I asked her to elaborate, and then she left."

"Oh my goodness." Jenny slowly stood, her mouth tumbling open. "I think I just found her."

We all turned and looked toward the front door.

Poppy looked gorgeous in a dark sheath dress, her hair perfectly curled, her eyes smoky. She was clearly ready to have a wonderful evening.

Summer rushed up. "Oh my God, Poppy brought Rafael!"

Sure enough, Poppy was beaming at a smiling Rafael, who was dressed in a black suit coat and a black button-up, a night-and-day contrast to his customary Giovanni's red-shirt uniform.

He led Poppy through the room by the elbow.

"When did she start dating him?" I asked, confused.

"My guess would be thirty seconds ago," Annabel said. "I have to hand it to her, it's a ballsy move. But I'm not sure Leo's the kind of guy this will work on. I'm thinking it won't motivate him to get off his butt and fight for her. It just might send him running."

Summer began to shake her hands like she had a secret to tell. "He might already be running, but in a different direction. I didn't want to ruin Poppy's big night, but Leo's ex has been threatening to show up to this for the past week. We finally found out what his distraction was, and it's her. Poppy's been right all along."

"What?" Jenny and I both gasped at the same time.

"Yeah," Summer said. "And we can't exactly keep Pamela out, because this event is open to the public. Leo's been a mess about it, but only told Xander yesterday. I couldn't bring myself to tell Poppy, just in case she decided not to show. But"—she nodded in the direction of the front door—"maybe Poppy found out on her own and decided to do something about it?"

"It's unknown, but I'm about to solve this crime," Annabel said. "I'm heading in." She began to walk toward her sister.

Marco stepped up behind me, his arm slipping around my waist as he whispered in my ear, "Who's Poppy with?"

"A server from Giovanni's who's had the hots for her for years."

"They actually make a stunning couple."

I wrapped my arms around him, happy he was going to be with me when the drama unfolded. Happy it wasn't our drama.

"They do. But he's not where her heart is. Whatever's going on here, we'll help her get through it."

He leaned over, kissing me. "She's lucky to have you."

"And I'm lucky to have you."

"No one is luckier than me."

Together, we were ready for whatever came next.

Singles in Seattle: Book 3

TITLE COMING

a novel

IVY DANIELS

Chapter 1

It was too late now. I was committed.

Or should *be* committed. The jury was out on that, but I was certain I'd have a rollicking consensus by the end of the evening.

I'd decided to take a leap. A big, fat, crazy leap of faith.

And, weirdly, I'd kept my very best friends in the world, along with my sister and her girlfriend, in the dark. I hadn't shared a single detail about my plans for the evening with any of them, which was so unlike me.

I blabbed everything, to everyone. Every barista in Seattle knew my tea. Every bartender knew my business. Every shopkeeper knew my style. I was an open book.

But not tonight. No one was getting a chance to tell me my plan sucked.

No, sirree.

Tonight, Leo was going to realize he couldn't live without

me. That I was the spot remover to his stain. The coffee bean to his latte. The lint roller to his tweed. The tiny, cute scissors to his perfectly trimmed beard.

We were meant to be together, and it was going to happen this evening.

After months of flirting and no action, of him acting weirder and weirder as we'd finished up the interior of Zoe's Lager, the brewpub he was opening tonight with his best friends Xander and Chris, I was done waiting. I'd reached my absolute threshold. Waiting was the eighth deadly sin.

Or maybe the ninth or tenth?

It didn't matter, because things were going to come to a head tonight, just as soon as I opened that door and walked—

"You look beautiful." Startled, I glanced at the man standing to my left. He smiled, flashing a set of very white teeth. "Like a princess. You know," he gestured with a curl of his fingers as he searched for the right word, "like from a Disney movie. But better, you know, more lively."

I blinked.

So, this wasn't a dream, then?

Much to my chagrin, I was actually standing on a regular street in Ballard, instead of floating around on a cloud somewhere in my wildest dreams. "Oh, thanks. This is my ride or die dress. I've had it forever, but I only break it out for special occasions." The tea length black sheath with a long slit up one leg contoured perfectly to my shape. I'd found it on a sales rack at a high-end department store three years ago, and literally jumped around clutching it to my chest like the rare gem that it was. A designer masterpiece at an affordable price that needed no alterations.

The elusive, yet highly exciting white whale.

I looked amazing in it.

Rafael, a waiter from Giovanni's, our favorite pizza place in Seattle, and my date for the evening, had broken through my contemplative reverie.

Better known as: The last chance to talk myself out of doing something really stupid.

He stood next to me looking cute in an Italian mafia sort of way. His chest hair curled out of his deeply unbuttoned shirt, which was thankfully hidden under a nice suit jacket. It was hard to ignore the glint of gold flashing between all the furriness, but overall it went with his vibe, so I couldn't complain. I'd told him that this was an important evening for me, so he'd dressed for it.

And it was.

Not only was I going to win Leo's affection, I was also making my big foray back into the interior design world.

A world I'd missed a lot more than I'd allowed myself to admit. Zoe's Lager was already getting rave reviews. I'd sunk my heart and soul into it. Every cell in my body had come together to create something I was incredibly proud to call my own. Design was where my heart was. I knew that now beyond a shadow of a doubt now.

The night should be about that, and that alone.

Instead, I was about to walk inside my crowning achievement with a waiter who'd had the hots for me for years, in a desperate bid to make the man of my dreams jealous.

Jealous enough that seeing me with another man would spur him into realizing he couldn't live without me. Best case scenario, he'd tear me out of Rafael's arms with unbridled fervor, vowing to love me forever in front of a crowd of two hundred plus people.

But more than likely, he'd escort me into the kitchen and profess his love next to the industrial refrigerator in a pocket just big enough for two of us.

It was nice and quiet back there.

After all that heroism, we would dramatically hop astride a white horse that I'd somehow Uber up, and we'd gallop off into the night for our happily ever after.

Upon reaching our final destination, which would most likely be a castle in some far-off land with lots of rolling hills and wild flowers, we'd have wild, multi-orgasmic sex for days and days, which would morph into months, and then finally years. We would remain blissfully happy, have a bevy of children, and be the kind of couple who held hands and stared into each other's eyes muttering sweet nothings until we reached our hundred birthdays, upon which we would die peacefully in each other's arms.

Why would I ever think that plan wouldn't work?

"Shall we go inside?" Rafael gestured toward the interior where people were imbibing and having a great time. I knew my family and friends were waiting for me, wondering where the hell I was. I should've been there to welcome the very first guest. I should've been in there setting up, rubbing elbows with Leo and flirting.

Instead, I was out here second-guessing myself.

This wasn't something Poppy Albright did on a regular basis. She was sure of herself to a fault. Absolutely bursting with self-confidence.

Honestly, it was a little annoying.

Me, her alter ego, Poppet, was not.

As much as I tried to keep Poppy in control, Poppet made an appearance every now and again. It couldn't be helped. Insecurity and trauma of past relationships had ways of resurfacing, no matter how hard you tried to tamp them down.

"Are you okay?" Rafael asked, his soothing Italian accent a balm to my stress and indecisiveness. "Would you like to go somewhere else?"

I shook my head like I'd finally broken the surface of a pool after holding my breath for a really long time. "No. I'm ready."

Was I? I guess we'd see.

Rafael opened the door. He went first, offering me his elbow.

I grabbed onto it like a lifeline, and to add to the legitimacy of the grift I was now running, I glanced up at him adoringly, fluttering my eyelashes and giggling.

Second, after my love of interior design, was acting, and I was frickin' *great* at it.

I just had to keep the lie going for a while.

Maybe an hour or two.

Sufficient enough time for Leo to don his knight in shining armor gear and escort me into the kitchen. He was going to look adorable in it, too. His thick, sandy blond hair would flow out the bottom of the helmet like a medieval hockey player. His nicely tapered waist, balanced by a pair of broad shoulders, would make more than a few heads turn. His greenish-hazel eyes peeking out of the face frame would make every woman within a three-mile radius want to weep.

Once he was ready, he'd come for me.

Poppet that was sure of it.

She was almost mostly never wrong.

"This place is stunning," Rafael commented.

I hadn't told him I'd been the one who'd designed it. We hadn't exactly had time to chitty-chat. I'd wandered into Giovanni's late last night high on Poppet's master plan. I'd made my move without a ton of consideration, asking him out as he'd shuffled a pizza paddle in and out of the brick oven.

He'd said yes, we exchanged numbers, and that had been the extent of it.

Asking him out may have been a move made out of desperation, but it'd been a move nonetheless.

"Thank you," I told him. "It's mine."

"Yours?"

I didn't have a chance to reply because my sister Annabel, the gorgeous Amazonian resident of our family, came rushing up to me, tugging my forearm. "Please excuse us," she told Rafael. "I need her for a teensy smidge." She held up her index finger and thumb. She hadn't waited for Rafael to acquiesce before she began dragging me across the room, hissing in my ear, "What do you think you're doing?"

"What you mean?"

I tried innocence first. Why not?

"You know exactly what I mean. Why would you bring the Giovanni's guy to your big opening?"

"Because I like him."

"You do not."

I settled my hands on my hips, annoyed for the eleventith million time that I had to glance *up* at my sister because I was short and she was tall. "I do, too. And I needed a date. This is a big night."

"It's a huge night. And you don't need a date."

We weren't arguing, but we weren't *not* arguing.

"I decided I needed a date."

She crossed her arms. "When? Thirty seconds ago?"

"How could I have asked him thirty seconds ago. That clearly would've been enough time—"

"Answer the question." She was not having it.

"Fine. I asked him out last night. And yes, I'm ecstatic about it. I'm here at my grand opening with a cute date and I'm about to have a very enjoyable evening."

"What about Leo?"

"What about him? The man has yet to notice I'm a living, breathing human being. I've done everything except jiggle my bare boobs at him." She did not want to know how close I'd come to doing that very thing. The man was a sexy beast who I wanted to sleep with who sucked at subtle hints. "He has no interest in me. I'm coming to terms with it. Rafael is helping."

Annabel dropped her arms in frustration. "I know you like I know myself, and your ploy isn't going to work. You're not going to make Leo jealous by hanging out on Italian Fabio's arm. He's going to retreat farther into his shell. He's a super shy guy. He's going to take this as a signal that you're not interested."

"He can't retreat any farther. He's already living across the entire ocean in some coral bed where shells live." I tried not to Muppet flail my arms, because attention was already on us. I could feel my girlfriends' eyeballs piercing into my soul. I loved them like a carnivore loved bacon, but they were going to have to let me do my thing tonight. "He either starts to paddle back, or he doesn't. Either way I'm determined to have fun at my own party. I deserve that."

Annabel's face softened. "Of course you do. I just don't want you to make a huge mistake. You've been into Leo for months."

"Leo and I are not a thing. We're not dating. We haven't been intimate. There have been no love words exchanged. He has not seen my nipples. I'm a free woman. And I haven't had a date in a full year. I'm done waiting."

Stephanie, Annabel's new super amazing semi-pro playing volleyball girlfriend, also from Themyscira, came up to us. "Hey. I hate to interrupt this sisterly lovefest, but you guys are becoming a focal point and I don't think either of you want that."

Without trying to be obvious, I turned my head a fraction of an inch and scanned the room. Sure enough, many unfamiliar faces, and a few very familiar ones, were staring right at us. Zapping back into my acting role like a director had yelled action, I reached out to give Stephanie a hug. I had to stand on my tiptoes. "Thank you for rescuing me from your persnickety girlfriend. You look beautiful tonight. Now if you both excuse me, I have to get back to my date."

"I hope you're doing the right thing," my sister said as she slipped her arm around Stephanie's waist.

"I am," I chirped, practically skipping back to Rafael. I hadn't seen Leo yet, but I knew he was around someplace. I chose to ignore my best friends for the time being.

What was I going to say to them? They would have similar views to Annabel and now was not the time.

I was committed.

This is what being committed looked like.

Rafael stood at the bar, which was the masterpiece of the entire brewpub. It commanded the center of a large two-story space. Porous, black soapstone reclaimed from a defunct salon was pieced together to perfection to achieve a continuous oval. It sat atop alternating corrugated metal and reclaimed redwood from a recent nineteen hundreds mansion teardown.

It was a shining star.

Five bartenders worked behind it, busting their butts pulling taps from thirty different spouts.

Buying materials like that at full price would've annihilated the budget. Instead, it came in a two grand under.

I was a miracle designer.

"What would you like to drink?" Rafael asked.

Before I could answer, Summer stood beside me, addressing the bartender, "She gets whatever she wants on the house."

I flashed her my thousand-megawatt smile. "You're the best, Summy!"

"Those instructions are straight from the top," she said. "I recommend trying a Summer Day Ale. It has hints of peach and ginger. Or maybe you'd prefer a Poppy's Perfection? It has undertones of honey and lemon."

We squealed as we hugged.

This was such a big day for both of us. Her hotty, salt-of-the-earth boyfriend owned this bar and she'd been with him from almost the beginning.

"I'm trying a Poppy's Perfection," I announced to the bartender. I'd met some of the staff while I was attending to last-minute details, but I hadn't met this one.

Once he handed it to me, I held it up to Summer, who raised her own, and we clinked glasses. I took a sip and *oohed* and *aahed*. It was amazing! Chris had been working on recipes for months. He'd hinted that he was going to name one after me, but I hadn't known which one.

I turned to Rafael, to introduce him to Summer. "Rafael, this is one of my best friends on the whole planet, Summer Day. Her boyfriend owns this place."

He reached across to shake Summer's hand. "Nice to finally meet you." He nodded. "I've seen you in the restaurant many times." Giovanni's had been our hang out since college.

"It's nice to finally meet you, too. Thank you for coming tonight," Summer replied graciously. I appreciated her not making a big deal that I was here with him. I knew what she was thinking, she didn't have to say it. She, of all people, knew how important Leo had been to me the past few months, because Xander and him were the very best of friends. "A reporter from the Seattle Gazette is here and she wants to interview you." She shook my forearm. "It's so exciting! Everybody is talking about the design. You managed to combine at least four different styles into one truly stunning visual." She was right. I had. The place was a mix of retro, mod, rustic, and chic. To achieve that feat, I'd papered the largest wall in gigantic pink zee's edged in silver for a retro 80s vibe, the other walls had been painted matte black to match the rustic bar. The booths alternated in green and purple velvet with a nod to the mod, and the lighting, tables and chairs were all chic with a few flouncy adornments in gold. A splash of gold never hurts.

It was all wrapped together in beautifully chocolate-stained reclaimed wide plank flooring with added windows for spectacular natural lighting.

"You're going to get so much work from this," Summer assured me.

I grabbed onto her hand. "I hope so! I'm all in on design. I loved every stinking minute of this." When Leo hadn't been acting weird. His distraction toward the end had been…well, distracting.

"Xander's waving me over to talk to someone. His entire family and all their friends are here, so I have to run. I'm sorry your parents couldn't make it. I was so looking forward to seeing them."

"My mom is so bummed, and my dad apologizes to me constantly. He broke his foot at the very wrong time. Surgery is next week, but they're planning to come up after he recovers. They promised."

"When they get here, we'll do a special dinner," she assured me, reaching over to give me a cheek kiss. Before she leaned back, she whispered, "I hope you know what you're doing. I love you."

Before I could reassure her that Poppet's plan was a slam dunk, she hustled away.

I called to her retreating back, "I love you, too!"

This plan was almost surely maybe going to work.

About the Author

Ivy Daniels lives in Minneapolis with her husband. She enjoys traveling, sunny beaches, and playing scrabble. She loves writing romantic comedy with a heave dose of humor. If you're interested in reading more, check out her website. She loves to hear from fans. Happy reading!

www.authorivydaniels.com

Stay tuned for more hilarous romantic comedy novels!

Sign-up for Ivy Daniel's Book Alert newsletter

so you don't miss a thing!

www.authorivydaniels.com

Nothing is completed without a great team.

My many thanks to:

Awesome Cover design: Estella Vukovic
Copyedits/proofs: Joyce Lamb
Final proof: Marlene Roberts